HER CLIENT
FROM HELL

BY
LOUISA GEORGE

MILLS & BOON

Published in Great Britain 2014
by Mills & Boon, an imprint of Harlequin (UK) Limited,
Eton House, 18-24 Paradise Road, Richmond, Surrey, TW9 1SR

© 2014 Louisa George

ISBN: 978 0 263 24210 2

Harlequin (UK) Limited's policy is to use papers that are natural,
renewable and recyclable products and made from wood grown in
sustainable forests. The logging and manufacturing processes conform
to the legal environmental regulations of the country of origin.

Printed and bound in Great Britain
by CPI Antony Rowe, Chippenham, Wiltshire

'Jack.' It was meant to be a warning. A definitive no. But it sounded like a whimper.

No, it sounded like an invitation. And maybe it was. Cassie didn't know. Didn't know anything, really—except that this man had stirred something in her that had long been dormant. Which was equal parts thrilling and scary. Actually, it was scary as hell.

Before she could breathe again Jack was in front of her, all six feet plus of impressiveness, his scent of heat and man filling her nostrils. His hard body... *there*. The open-necked shirt revealing just a little of a tanned chest that she suddenly wanted to touch, his smile now almost blossoming.

The street seemed to fade out a little as her vision narrowed to just him. His hand was on her cheek, the lightness of his touch making her heart stutter. The intensity in his eyes caused her abdomen to contract with a need she hadn't expected.

This was utter crazyville. A choc chip short of a cookie. How could she want to slap him and kiss him at the same time? He was pompous and a giant pain in the neck...and she wanted to kiss him.

No. No. No.

Yes.

Dear Reader

After deciding to write a book we're often told to *write what you know*, but with this book I got a chance to write what I love too! My heroine Cassie is a chef and, while I am far from the proverbial domestic goddess, I do absolutely adore food, so it was a real treat to be able to indulge that passion throughout Cassie's story and have a little fun with it along the way!

I also love carnival time and dancing, so setting some scenes at the famous Notting Hill Carnival in London meant I could reminisce a little about my experiences there too—I hope I've captured some of the magic of this amazing event.

We met Cassie Sweet in my first Modern Tempted™ book, BACKSTAGE WITH HER EX, where we discovered that she is a woman who just wants to have fun and takes life less than seriously. What could be better, then, than for her to meet her match in Jack Brennan, who is the ultimate in serious?

Now Cassie is trying to make a go of her catering business—under a certain amount of financial pressure—so she has to impress the unimpressable Jack in order to win a catering contract, while trying to ignore the pull of an intense attraction. Jack, meanwhile, is not interested in having any kind of deep and meaningful relationship, especially with a woman like Cassie, so watching these two struggling with the sizzling tension is a real delight (authors can be so mean!).

I love writing for the Modern Tempted series—the characters are so fresh and real and fun. I hope you enjoy reading about them too.

For all my writing news and release dates visit me at www.louisageorge.com

Happy reading!

Louisa x

Having tried a variety of careers in retail, marketing and nursing (where a scratchy starched uniform was mandatory), **Louisa George** is now thrilled that her dream job of writing for Harlequin Mills & Boon® means she gets to go to work in her pyjamas.

Originally from Yorkshire, England, Louisa now lives in Auckland, New Zealand, with her husband, two sports-mad teenage sons and two male cats. Writing romance is her opportunity to covertly inject a hefty dose of pink into her heavily testosterone-dominated household.

When she's not writing or reading Louisa loves to spend time with her family and friends, enjoys travelling, and adores eating great food (preferably cooked by someone else). She's also hopelessly addicted to Zumba®.

Visit her at www.louisageorge.com

Other Modern Tempted™ titles by Louisa George:

BACKSTAGE WITH HER EX

**This and other titles by Louisa George
are available in eBook format
from www.millsandboon.co.uk**

To Warren, my carnival partner
and failed recipe attempt victim,
your support means everything to me.

Happy anniversary!
Thanks for the last 20 years—here's to another 20!

I love you x

CHAPTER ONE

Sweet Treats Website Contact Form,
10th August, 9.55p.m.
Hi! How can Sweet Treats help you?

Contact from: JB@zoom.co.uk
I need catering for a wedding party of 50 (fifty)
adults (no children) on 6th September. Better in-
clude some vegan options. Nothing too 'out there'.
(Neither too trendy nor endangered).
Send menu suggestions ASAP.
I hope your food is better than your website.
JB

Whoa, someone was in serious need of a happy pill.

Cassie Sweet squeezed the bridge of her nose, closed her eyes and wondered what the hell she'd done that was so bad she had to endure this.

Impossible clients. 1: Like *JB@zoom*. At way too late o'clock, making rude comments about her business. 2: People who said things and then explained them in brackets.

Impossible choices. Her regular no-holds-barred mojito night with the girls struck out for a mind-distorting evening in front of the laptop trying to magic her business out of financial chaos.

And *impossible decisions*. Instead of telling JB where to stick their rude comments, she'd have to smile sweetly and reply positively. It was a job and, even though her work schedule was overflowing, one glance at her bank statement told her there were far too many minus signs. Looked as if she didn't have a choice.

Email to: JB@zoom.co.uk
Well, hi, JB. Are you Mr? Miss? Dr? Rev? Lord?

Cassie resisted the temptation to add *Sith?*

Congratulations on your upcoming wedding!
Sweet Treats would be happy to help. Please find en-
closed a copy of our specials menu and suggested
vegan options for three, four and five courses. Please
don't hesitate to contact me for further info. I'm more
than happy to talk things over.
Cassie
For Sweet Treats

She looked back down at the spreadsheet and willed the red numbers to be black. Damn her stupid trusting genes. She was way too much like her father; there was no doubt that William Sweet's too-trusting blood definitely ran through her veins.

The figures swam in and out of focus. One day she'd been financially stable and then...wham! Sucker-punched by betrayal. She would never trust a man again.

Except, perhaps, for her bank manager, who she would not only trust but would love for ever if he could help her work a way out of this. Or maybe the bank manager was a woman? Who knew?

Her ex, actually. He'd set up the accounts with Cassie's

signature and apparent blessing. She, meanwhile, had focused on the catering side, giving little attention to running the business.

Well, hell, she was paying attention now. And oh, it would be so easy to run to her family and ask for help, but this time—*this time*—she was going to prove them all wrong. She did have stickability. She could cope without them.

Unlike her failed dog-walking business…her brief foray as a children's entertainer…or the blip that was her disastrous market stall—why the hell they had to have them so early in the morning she didn't know. This time she was going alone and this time she would succeed.

Her mobile rang. *Blocked number.*

Glancing at the clock, she breathed in, fists curling in anticipation. What time was it in deepest, conveniently out of killing distance, South America? By the time she'd finished with him, his number wouldn't be the only thing that was blocked.

Picking up, she kept her voice steady. 'Patrick, if that's you I swear I'm going to take out my paring knife and chop your—'

'Hey, hey. Steady, lady. Put. The. Knife. Down.' The voice, so not her ex's, was deep and dusky, a little tired at the edges. Like her. It wasn't a posh accent per se—definitely London. Did she mention dusky?

'I'm not Patrick. And even if I were I wouldn't admit to it now.'

'Believe me, if you were Patrick you wouldn't have a breath left in your body.' Although, three months down the line, she'd given up hope of seeing him or her money again. Case closed, they'd said.

'Oh? A woman scorned?'

She supposed she was. Her ex hadn't so much broken

her heart as completely stamped on every trusting fibre in her body. 'Who is this?'

'Jack Brennan. I just got your email with suggestions.'

Not the ones she was really thinking. Such an unexpectedly warm voice for one so rude.

'Oh, hello. Yes. My food is great; I come highly recommended. You saw the testimonial page?'

'Eventually. Does it need to be so busy? I couldn't find anything; it's definitely not user-friendly. There are too many tabs. Too many options.'

Well, really? Mr Sexy Voice had become Mr Cocky and Irritating in the blink of an eye. Maybe she wasn't so desperate that she needed to add his job to her already overflowing schedule.

Yes, she was. 'Thanks for the feedback. I'll make a note and consider a re-jig of my website next time I have an advertising budget.' Like never. Raising her head above the cyberworld parapet and reminding the webmaster of her existence, and therefore her unpaid overdue bill, would only cause more trouble. 'I guess it could do with a spruce.'

'It needs a deforestation.'

Like your manners. 'As it happens, the website detail belonged to my…er…ex-business partner. I'm making changes. It takes time.'

'Your ex-partner and Patrick—I presume they're the same person?'

'Yes, he was the brains behind the business, allegedly. I'm the chef.'

'Private party? Personal chef. Yes—'

'Please don't make any comments about that byline. I came up with it, and I like it.' It was about the only thing she had left. *Apart from my dignity*, and that was starting to sag a little round the edges too.

But that voice… How could someone so rude sound

so hot? It was like chocolate velvet, wrapping her up and making parts of her warm that hadn't been warm in quite a while.

Which was a stark enough reminder that this was business. Hadn't she learnt already never to mix that with pleasure?

And she was not that desperate to flirt with a client *who was getting married*. It was just a voice.

'So, considering your late call, I presume you are interested in using Sweet Treats for the wedding? Have you had a look at the menu options? I'm happy to juggle things around if you want to mix and match.'

'I don't know. It's complicated. We need to meet and discuss this further. And time's running out.' She wondered how easy it was for him to speak without the aid of brackets to explain everything in duplicate. A hum of traffic buzzed in the background. He raised his voice. 'How about tomorrow? Afternoon? Evening?'

'I'll just check.' Looking at her diary, she worked out she could fit him in between Zorb's regular Friday Feast lunch order, little Hannah's third birthday party and the carnival meeting early Saturday morning. Couldn't she? Sleep was seriously overrated. As was a social life.

As for a sex life? She literally laughed. Out loud. Sex was something she remembered from her dim and distant past. Vaguely. *Hell*, twenty-six and sex was just a memory? If she planned right, she could fit in a quickie between the hours of three and four in the morning. Next Wednesday week. But, in her experience, most guys weren't particularly happy with that. Well, not the kind of guys she wanted to spend that special hour with, anyway.

Better make that two people in need of a happy pill. 'I can fit you in at around six-thirty. Would that work? Where are you based?' She jotted down the details. 'Actually, you're just down the road from me; I'm in Notting Hill too. When the business started to take off we decided to move—'

He sighed. 'Look, I'm in a cab; it's hard to hear. I don't need your life story. I just need food.'

'Of course. Of course.' *Tetchy.* She hadn't quite mastered the art of managing her thoughts in silence. Or managing anything at all, really, outside the kitchen. But she was trying hard. 'I usually meet my clients at Bean in Notting Hill Gate, just a few shops down from the cinema. It's a sort of café-bar, open office space for independent professionals. I'll hire a meeting room so we can chat in relative privacy. There are also office facilities there in case we need any photocopying et cetera. If that suits your requirements, Mr Brennan?'

'Perfectly.' His growl wasn't nearly as scary as he intended. 'This is my first time at organising a wedding breakfast and I want to get it right. I've absolutely no intention of doing it again.'

'I'm sure Mrs Brennan-to-be will be very glad to hear that.'

'What?' Some tooting and a curse from a voice that wasn't dark and rich interrupted the conversation. Then he was back. 'Sorry?'

Cassie spoke slowly. 'Your intended? Mrs Brennan-to-be. Will she be joining us tomorrow? I find that it cuts down on problems and saves a lot of everyone's time if the happy couple thrash out ideas and differences way before the event. So I'd prefer to meet you both. Tomorrow. If that's okay?'

There was a pause. Then, 'There is no Mrs Brennan-to-be.'

Ah. She knew it—that deep voice was way too good

to be heterosexual. 'Oh. Sorry. Er...well, bring *Mr* Brennan-to-be along.'

'No. No. No. Not at all. I'll explain tomorrow...er...?' She imagined him sitting in the back of a cab, squinting through a monocle at her business card, trying to make out the name of the woman he was phoning.

'Cassie,' she reminded him. No wife? No husband. 'Erm...you're not one of those marrying his pet iguana kind of guys, are you? I mean, I'm not one to judge, but I'm not sure what iguanas eat.'

He laughed. Finally. Hesitant—reluctant, even, but there. Free for a moment, unctuous like thick, warm chocolate ganache. Or was it just a gasp? Whichever, it was gone as quickly as it appeared. 'I have no intention of marrying a man or an iguana. Or anyone, for that matter, Cassie. Yes. Short for Cassandra?'

'Says the guy who doesn't want my life story.' But now she really, really wanted his. Although she wasn't surprised such a grumpy, tetchy man hadn't got a wife-to-be or a husband and was only appealing to a reptile.

But she really, really needed his money.

There was another toot of a horn, his voice fading in and out. 'Tomorrow, then. Oh, and one more thing.'

'Yes?'

'Leave the paring knife at home.'

This had to be the weirdest conversation she'd ever had. Organising a wedding breakfast for a man who wasn't getting married. Maybe he'd had his heart broken and couldn't move on? Maybe he was channelling Miss Havisham? Tragic.

And that was definitely none of her concern. Because she was not going to allow any man to wheedle his way into her business or her heart—*especially* her heart—ever again.

* * *

Jack Brennan jogged down the steps of his Notting Hill home and checked his watch—time minus twenty minutes. What the hell he was doing he didn't know. But if he could organise a film crew to shadow a rock group across twenty European music festival venues at the drop of a hat, he could organise a few flimsy sandwiches.

No.

His heart squeezed a little. Lizzie was not getting sandwiches for her wedding. He'd make damned sure of that. She deserved a whole lot better, whether she liked it or not. He just had to find the time—and courage—to tell her.

A wall of noise greeted him as he opened the door to Bean. The café was filled with the Friday after-work-before-dinner crowd. With standing room only, he was grateful that the scatty-sounding Cassie had shown a little foresight to book a room, because discussing the finer points of canapés across this racket would be impossible. Still, the food smelt of something exotic and spicy—garlic, chilli and coriander—sending his stomach into a growling fit, and he remembered he hadn't eaten. Editing his current documentary had taken up the majority of his afternoon. Food had, as always, taken a back seat.

Ten minutes later he was still standing there, blood pressure escalating. Unused to being stood up, looked over or generally let down these days, he made for the exit. Cassie Sweet had had her chance. If she couldn't make it on time for the initial meeting, how could he trust her to be reliable for the event? The event he needed so badly to be a success.

As he reached for the handle the door swung almost off its hinges and a blur of colour rushed in. 'Hey—Mr Brennan? Jack? Are you Jack? I'm Cassie.'

'You're late.'

'I know—I'm sorry. I tried to call but reception was

patchy—' She dug deep into a large battered brown satchel that looked like a relic from way before his school days and pulled out a phone and showed him it. 'I got held up with a client at a birthday party. There was an emergency and I just couldn't leave her with all those children.'

From the phone call last night and what he knew about chefs—which was diddly-squat—he'd conjured up an image of an older, larger, bitter woman, hair piled up on her head exposing two fat ruddy cheeks and small glittering eyes. Okay, so what he knew about chefs amounted to a TV reality show about some Scottish bloke swearing in a sweat-filled steel kitchen and the overly cuddly nineteen-twenties period drama below-stairs cook.

Wrong. So damned wrong on every level.

A twinkle in her eye, yes. A cocky mouth, yes. But he hadn't imagined such a mouth—teasing and smiling. Lips that were full and covered with a slick of something shimmery and red. Pinned-up hair, yes. But secured with a pair of chopsticks on the top of her head, with wisps of vibrant auburn corkscrewing at angles round her face.

Something glittered on her cheek, a smudge that sparkled—he thought for a moment about pointing it out. But it kind of went with the whole chaotic look.

And curves, yes. Very interesting, framed by a bright loose-fitting top in dazzling browns and blues and oranges, the kind of thing an old-fashioned gypsy might wear, secured by a thick dark brown belt. Below that, a layered frilly white skirt ended just above her knees. On her feet she wore flat leather laced tan sandals. All Greek goddess meets hippy. A crazy artsy type with her head in the stars. So not his type. A pretty head, though, porcelain skin. And that hair...

As wild and crazy as she was.

This whole escapade was already shifting him way too

far out of his comfort zone; he didn't need a too-hot boho airhead added to the mix. Regardless of the curves and the hair…and the curves…

He shook his head. 'Well, I'm sorry. You've had your chance; I'm leaving.'

'Oh. But we haven't even—' Her mouth turned downwards, her hand on his arm. 'Please don't. I did try to call…'

'I don't have time to be wasted. Nate said you were reliable. And keen.' Frazzled more like, as if she was juggling a zillion things in the air and they were all dropping around her. But she was still smiling and he was drawn to that, in some kind of weird masochistic way.

So she was pretty. Didn't mean a thing. Certainly didn't mean the woman could cook.

Nate had also mentioned she'd been babied during a difficult upbringing, that she'd had little direction in her life apart from partying and that she was trying to prove herself with this catering venture. She'd already dabbled at other things like…nannying, was it? Dog-walking? And lost not only cash but interest far too quickly.

Nate hadn't mentioned anything about an ex-business partner, though, or the need for a paring knife. So Jack guessed Cassie kept her family in the dark about some things.

Which suddenly made her a whole lot more interesting. In a purely professional way. Teasing dark secrets from people had made him a stack of money and cemented his reputation as the best gritty documentary maker in the UK.

'So Nate told you about me?' Two pink patches on her cheeks darkened to red. 'Nate Munro? I wondered…usually people use a search engine or a business card rather than a world famous rock star to find a caterer.'

'Yes, he recommended you. Although why I bothered

I don't know—' But his new mate had done him a huge honour by allowing him to film his more intimate home life for a documentary which could well be award-winning—if only for the usually very private subject. Which meant Jack owed him precisely five more minutes to hear Cassie out before he took his leave and found a more organised, punctual and less disturbingly off-the-scale attractive caterer.

The flush turned from embarrassment to irritation. She wore her emotions very obviously on her face—as if there was no caution button. No keeping things in check. How could people live like that? Spilling their feelings out at any given moment? Did they have no control? It was his endless fascination and what made his films so damned compelling to watch.

'Nate's almost as bad at interfering in my life as his wife. That's my sister, Sasha. I keep telling them to butt out and I know they mean well, but...' She inhaled deeply and breathed out slowly. 'But, well, you've already said you don't want my life story.'

'I already know Nate's, and a little of your sister's... and therefore some of yours.'

'Not the best bits.' She winked, but he refused to laugh. He did not want to know about the best bits of her life. Or the worst. Or anything more about her. Five minutes. Her hands moved as she talked. Was there not a serene molecule in that far too interesting body? 'So you're the rockumentary producer man—my sister did mention you. And Nate's right; I am reliable. I've just been having a trying time recently.'

'Yes.' He tried to keep up. 'Something about a paring knife?'

'I left it at home. Which is probably a good thing, seeing as you look like you might want to use it.' She stuck out her hand. 'Okay. Can we begin again? I'm Cassie Sweet. Caterer extraordinaire. And just a little bit out of control right now. But normal service is being resumed. And my cooking is brilliant.' She smiled.

'Jack Brennan.' *Always in control*. He shook her hand. It was warm and soft. And why the hell he'd even noticed he didn't know.

She took a step back and looked around at the crowd, then raised her voice above the chattering. 'I've booked a room. Hang on a sec.' She turned to speak to a passing waitress, who shook her head and shrugged.

'Shoot.' Cassie sighed loudly and her fist curled tight around the satchel strap. Was that a curse under her breath? 'They gave the room to someone else because I was late.'

Typical. This escapade was turning into a disorganised farce. He needed to leave and take his chances on someone more professional. 'Look. Forget it. I'll find someone else. Some time else.'

'No. Please. Please. Tell me this isn't happening.'

'It is. In full glorious Technicolor.' *Your problem, my nightmare.*

'I'll have a word with Frankie, the manager. He's just over there.' Shoving her bag at Jack, she disappeared into the crowd. 'Frankie! Hey, Frankie!'

Did she have another speed? Like just plain old fast instead of whirlwind? And now he couldn't leave unless he took the bag with him or left it here. Unattended, in a crowded bar. It could end up in anyone's hands. And not that she didn't deserve it, but he didn't need that on his conscience. It was full enough already.

In a few moments she was back, breathless but grinning. 'Good old Frankie. There are a couple of free tables outside. Saves those for his best clients. Talking about food always makes me hungry so I've ordered some nibbles. They do the best soft shell tacos here with pork belly crackling. You must not leave without trying those. And he gave us a bottle of red on the house for the mix-up. Result!'

She brushed past him and Jack caught a scent of vanilla sugar and something distinctly soft and pretty, which he dutifully followed, trying not to watch the sway of her hips as she walked. Her backside looked just about the perfect size for his hands—jeez, he swallowed. Hard. What the hell was wrong with him?

With her? No caution or stop button. She was at warp speed. And now he was caught up in her chaos too.

So much for the five-minute plan. He blinked as he entered a small courtyard. Ivy, intertwined with scarlet flowers, curled over the walls, white gravel covered the ground. Small iron tables dressed with lit tea light candles dotted the space. It was like a secret garden from a movie he'd seen as a kid. Back when he'd believed in fairy tales like family and happy ever after. 'This is impressive.'

'Glad you like it. I wasn't sure if you'd think it was too...*out there*.' She raised her fingers and did quotation marks with them to emphasise her words, and he caught a teasing twinkle in her smile.

Then her eyes met his—darkest blue and wide and honest—and she seemed, for a moment, a little startled, but she didn't turn away. His heart thumped in his chest as he was drawn into that gaze, sucked deep and then deeper, and deeper still, as if he was tumbling somehow, like Alice down the rabbit hole.

A blush hit her cheeks again and she shook her head, breaking a tentative connection that left him feeling a little unnerved.

Opening her satchel, she pulled out a thick creamy notepad and folder of papers. 'Okay. Right. Let's get started. We have a lot to get through.' As she opened the folder a gust of wind caught the top sheets and sent them spiralling into the air. 'Oh, wait… Sorry. Oh, no, I can't believe this is happening. I'm sorry.'

Next, she was on her feet chasing the papers, stamping on a few to stop them floating away like confetti on the gentle breeze, more tendrils of her hair falling from the chopsticks.

He watched for a moment until it became clear he either helped or he'd be sitting here all night waiting for her to switch to simmer.

'Here you go.' He handed her the papers and she placed them back on the table and weighted them down with a large bowl of delicious-looking silky stuffed olives.

Popping one in her mouth, she bit down and smiled. 'Not just delicious, but useful too. Thanks. So not my day.' Finally she sat, took a long deep breath and slowed to a mode Jack could follow. She smiled again. She had a lot of them—endless smiles. Polite smiles. Embarrassed but intriguing smiles. Smiles that didn't quite hit her eyes. He got the impression she was trying very hard to be professional and thought that smiling would be the way to go.

But endless cheerfulness wouldn't convince him she'd be any good at helping him—and he needed help right now. Reliable. Organised. Straightforward help. 'Er…the wedding? Are we going to cover that tonight?'

'The wedding. Okay. Yes.' She leaned forward and there was the scent of vanilla sugar again. Sweet and soft. 'So, talk me through the day, Jack. Can I call you Jack? What's planned? What do you need?'

Hell if he knew. Now she'd actually focused, he suddenly felt way out of his depth. This was a stupid idea. He should have asked first instead of *interfering*…as Cassie had so succinctly described honest and well-meaning sibling interest.

He spoke slowly to give himself time to think and to engage her full attention. 'As I said, it's in three weeks' time. I'm not a hundred per cent sure of exact timings so I'll get back to you on that. The wedding ceremony is going to be in a community art space off Portobello Road. It's a small gathering of friends; there's an Irish band booked in the evening. The details are being finalised.'

She tucked one of the errant curls behind her ear. 'It's very short notice but, luckily, I do have space in my calendar. Tell me, though, you've waited until now to sort out the food because...?'

'I've just got back from filming; my schedule got changed a little.' And he'd been too damned busy to pay much attention to Lizzie's emails. Plus the word *help* had never been in her vocabulary. Even when she'd needed it the most. And he was, apparently, the world's worst at working out what women wanted. Why they didn't just straight out tell him, he didn't know. But he wanted to make this work, wanted to make her happy. After everything they'd been through, Lizzie deserved a slice of that.

Another smile. 'Okay, well, I guess we can work out some of the finer points later, but it would be useful if we could make a start on menu choices, just a jumping off point. I like to get a feel for the couple, their likes and tastes and dreams. Do you have a memorable meal you'd like to recreate? A theme?'

'Why all the deep and meaningful stuff? It's just food, right?' Clearly, there was a whole lot more to weddings than he'd ever given thought to. Actually, he'd never given thought to weddings at all—only that he'd never be having one. 'I...er...'

'Okay, no worries. Let's try a different angle.' Her eyes

twinkled through a confused frown. 'Tell me more about the iguana—was it love at first sight?'

It was the first time in a long time a woman had left him speechless.

CHAPTER TWO

'IT'S MY SISTER'S wedding. I'm organising the food, the car and the photographer.' Jack Brennan had an edge to him, a rippling intensity, brooding, which made Cassie immediately want to make him laugh.

Or at least smile. But somehow she didn't think he'd take kindly to a tickle in the ribs. He didn't look the type of guy who'd take kindly to much that wasn't serious and Very Important.

So what if he was? As she looked at him, all the breath sucked out of her lungs. Tall, and underneath that open-necked grey shirt he looked sculpted out of lean muscle with broad shoulders wide enough to tuck herself into. Dark tousled hair that made her fingers itch to ruffle some more. Deep brown eyes softened the defined features of his sharp cheekbones and square jaw. So what if he was cover-model gorgeous? Looks didn't make a man. That, she knew first-hand. This one was grumpy and grouchy and in need of a damn good belly laugh.

She put this over-the-top attention to his detail down to the dating drought she'd enforced until she wrestled her finances into some sort of order. Not even an extraordinarily hot man would distract her.

If only something today could actually go according to her well-constructed plan. Flighty and chaotic was not the impression she'd intended to give him. 'Well, that's very nice of you. What does your sister want as regards food? Brunch? Sit-down dinner? Buffet? Food stations? How many courses?'

'Whoa. Too many choices. Food stations? What the hell? I just want food. Good food. On a table, in a room. It's not rocket science.'

'No, it's not.' She tried to make the sigh escaping her lips sound a little less irritated. This was going to take a lot longer than she'd anticipated. Beauty he might have been, but empathetic he definitely was not. 'It is her *wedding* day.'

'Yes, I am fully aware of that, believe me.' He shook his head, his palms held up, and he had the decency to look a little embarrassed. 'Okay. Look, I'm coming clean. I am way out of my depth here. I didn't ask her what she wants to eat. She doesn't know I'm arranging this.'

'What? She doesn't know? How can someone organise food for a wedding without consulting the bride?' Answer: the man who spoke in brackets. Figured. But she bit back what she was truly thinking. Honesty didn't always go down well and she didn't want to jeopardise his wedding party of fifty and its very welcome boost to her finances.

He gave a nonchalant shrug of those magnificent shoulders. Which she noted purely for their potential ability to carry things. Heavy pans. Trays. She might need assistance on the day. Briefly. 'She said she was going to do it herself, she has a plan—and it's terrible. I can't let it happen.' At her frown he elaborated, 'Paying for the food is going to be my gift to her, a surprise.'

'Oh, it'll be a surprise all right. But not necessarily a good one. Fair play to you for wanting to help, but this isn't the right way to do it.' If there was one thing Cassie knew well it was that siblings often had great intentions but execution of intent wasn't always brilliant. Killing with kindness sprang to mind. Suffocation. Never being taken seriously. Plain old interfering. 'This may be news to you, but women tend to have a pretty definite opinion about what will happen on their wedding day. That usually includes the food too. And what about the husband? Did you ask him?'

'Callum? Why? He's a man. So long as there's plenty to eat he won't care what it is.'

'Gosh, you're all hearts and flowers, Mr Brennan, aren't you? And they say romance isn't dead.'

Was he for real? Thank God this was purely business because he was everything she kept away from. Overbearing. Too smart. Unfeeling. She usually went for the more laid-back type. And okay, well, the type you couldn't trust. But if she was ever thinking of dating again—which she wasn't—Jack's type would be at the bottom of her list.

Which was long.

So why, when he was clearly every shade of wrong, did her tummy lurch at the merest hint of a smile? It was very disconcerting.

She hid one of her own behind her surprise. Unlucky girl whoever fell for him—there'd be no wooing, or wining and dining. No riding off into the sunset or valentine's cards.

He shifted uncomfortably in his seat, crossing his legs. 'Personally, I don't believe in wasting time on fairy tales.' Something simmered behind those dark brown eyes—a depth that she hadn't been ready for. Hurt, maybe. Pain? Then it was gone in another quick shake of his head. 'But Lizzie's happy, I suppose.'

'Not for much longer once she's got wind of your plan to sabotage her wedding breakfast.' He seemed a little shocked by the notion that his sister could be happy, or was it that she was happy to be getting married that seemed so unpalatable? 'And you're planning to tell her that you've taken away her choice for food…when, exactly?'

His hand ran along his stubbled chin, the dark shadow creating a dangerous edge to his striking features. She got the impression he was used to getting his own way and not being challenged. Well, unlucky. Part of the success of a wedding day was the quality of the food; she wouldn't allow him to jeopardise that for his sister's sake or risk Sweet Treats' reputation by taking part in a fiasco. Her business depended largely on positive word of mouth or all her hard work would have been for nothing.

She sensed his irritation rising as that smooth deep voice took on a harder tone. 'Let's reframe this, shall we? I haven't taken away her choice, I'm going to free up her time, remove some stress and help her enjoy her special day.' The way he said *special* made Cassie believe he didn't think there was anything valuable in a lifetime commitment, just a whole host of stupid. 'I'll present her with my plan *when* I've decided who is going to be my caterer.'

'You're interviewing others?'

His perfect lips curled upwards at the edges. He had a kind of reluctant smile that was almost there, almost whole, but somehow stopped short. Cassie wondered what stopped it from fully blossoming. 'Of course. I have two lined up for tomorrow morning. I always keep my options very open.'

'I bet you do. Good idea. Excellent plan. But no one's going to agree to taking on a contract unless they have more concrete details this close to the day. Seriously, she might hate my ideas, or at the very least have some pretty fixed ones of her own.'

'Sandwiches. Quiche. Something God-awful called *quinoa,* which sounds more like a tropical disease than anything edible.' He visibly shivered. 'If I stood back and let her loose on that it'd be the worst wedding ever.'

'Forgive me for saying this, Mr Brennan, but with a bossy brother interfering behind her back it already is.' If she didn't take control he'd be bossing her too. Forthrightness was next to sound business, right? 'Now, I've printed these off thinking you might not have had time to look at them. I'm going to talk you through some ideas, on the proviso you go right back and tell her about the options available.'

Carefully opening the folder in case they blew away again, she gave him copies of her menu suggestions and ignored the black look he threw her. 'I've done a few quirky weddings in the past, themed receptions...anything goes, really. Some really embrace the idea of a breakfast, offering waffles and pancakes, French crepes, homemade pop tarts with hearts baked in them, that kind of thing. At the other end of the spectrum, cocktails are popular at the moment too, and local produce is a big hit.'

'Like jellied eels, pie and mash—that kind of thing?' The brown in his eyes glittered with hints of gold, which she imagined would be quite attractive. In another lifetime. On a more smiley man.

'If it floats your boat—you'd be surprised how many people do ask for it. Oh, but if you decide on food stations I'll have to hire a few other people—I can't wok and grill at the same time.'

His eyebrows rose. 'You do surprise me.'

'I can hire in waiter service from the local catering college to save cash if you go for that option. Although family-style is pretty on-trend too.' There she was, trying damned hard to be businesslike and professional, but those eyes....

He dropped the menus on to the table and shook his

head. 'You're blinding me with science. What's family-style?'

'Where the party sits at one large table and passes the food around to each other. You know, like a regular family dinner.'

'Oh. Of course. A regular family.' His gaze dipped down; he seemed to be pulling a thought or a memory from a distant place. Not a happy one. And something in her heart melted just a little. When he looked at her again his eyes were clear and bright and any vestige of emotion had fled. 'Don't you just have a set thing for the clueless? Wedding 101?'

'No.' She found her best smile. 'We believe in choice at Sweet Treats.'

An eyebrow peaked. 'We? Please don't tell me there are more of you?'

'Sorry. *I*,' she corrected herself. 'I'm adjusting to a new regime. It's just me. And that's really exciting.' If she said it enough times it might even come true.

'Maybe if you took a little time to crank down a gear or two. Slow to a more manageable speed?'

'Yes, well...' That would be lovely. Luxury. At least a pace where she could breathe and take stock, plan past tomorrow. But it wouldn't happen this side of Christmas. Or even this side of the decade. If she stopped, her business would die and she'd lose her apartment, along with her self-respect.

Sometimes she felt as if everything was teetering on a knife-edge. She tried to hide the flush of panic but it rolled through her, like it did sometimes in the dead of night, wakening her with a thick cold weight in her chest, and especially when she stared at those rows of numbers that made little sense.

So, whatever else happened, she had to keep him on

side—or, rather, keep him on the side of twenty-nine pounds a head times fifty. 'I'm managing just fine.'

'Really? Which school of customer relations did you attend? Because you might want to ask for your money back.' He smoothed his hand across his jaw, all the time keeping his dark eyes on hers. 'Being late is just fine? Losing a booked table is just fine? Keeping a client waiting is just fine?'

So he didn't speak in brackets, he just repeated things. Over and over to make his point. She got it now.

'No. Not at all.' She cleared her throat. She was trying her hardest, dammit. 'This afternoon I made three dozen red velvet cupcakes, decorated a fairy castle birthday cake and prepared finger food for twenty-two toddlers with every allergy imaginable. Then I drove over to Kilburn and presented them to a very happy and satisfied customer. Who then fell in the backyard and split her head wide open. What would you have liked me to do? Leave her to bleed out? Happy birthday, little Hannah, sorry about the concussion but I have to go because I have an appointment with a man who doesn't know what he wants for a sister who doesn't know he's doing it?'

Jack took a slug of wine and looked at her; something in his stance stiffened. 'No, of course not.'

She leaned back in her chair. 'Apology accepted.'

'I— That wasn't an apology...'

'Well, it should have been.'

'This is getting nowhere.' He stood up.

Scraping her chair back, she stood and faced him. Or at least faced his buttoned-up, Italian cotton-shirted rock-solid chest that looked just perfect to lean against, and peered up at his taut jaw and narrowed eyes. Then remembered some of the cardinal rules of customer service that

Patrick had drummed into her, back when he wasn't embezzling. Or maybe he already was.

Keep them happy. Jack didn't look happy.

Fulfil promises. She'd been late, and the room had been given away, and the wind had blown everything…

Go above and beyond. She'd done it for Hannah. But not for Jack Brennan.

And so that was it—not one tick in any of those boxes—and she'd bet anything Jack Brennan was the box-ticking type. He was angry because of her and she'd lost the job. Hurrah. Things just kept getting better.

It was hard. Running her business was hard. Saving her business was harder still. She tried to smile. But none came. Nothing. She didn't have any left.

In that moment the stress of the day—her life—boiled up inside her, too raw and fresh to hold back. 'Of course I was concerned about keeping you waiting. My business is my first priority and my clients are everything to me. But really? You have no idea how hard I'm trying and it feels like some days I'm going backwards. The cooking's fine and a real hit, but I couldn't help the head injury. And I squeezed you in when I probably should have made an appointment for a different day, but I didn't want to lose this chance.'

He opened his mouth to speak but she got in first, hearing her voice rising, louder and more high-pitched, but with no way to stop it. 'I have to do everything now—the ordering, the admin, the delivering. I don't have time to do the little stuff. But then suddenly I find out that the little stuff is actually quite important. Things like VAT and tax…'

'Very important, actually. Keeps the world going round. Now, if you'll excuse me?' He turned away, his back rigid as he took a step across the gravel.

'No. Stop. Wait. You probably have no idea how hard

it is to prove yourself to people. To have a dream that you want to take a chance on…and you have it there, almost in your grasp. Then someone comes along and snatches it all away. Have you ever had someone steal your dreams, Jack?'

That seemed to have an effect. He stopped abruptly and turned round, taking his time to face her. He studied her for a moment, which made her hot and cold at the same time. Suddenly she felt totally exposed in front of someone who kept his emotions clearly locked away because there was no way she could tell what he was thinking.

Finally, he spoke. 'Okay. I'm listening.'

'I just need a chance.'

'And I just need food.'

Not your life story. I know. 'I can do food. I can do damn good food.' She stopped talking then as she realised her voice was actually shaking, and he didn't need to know all of this. He just wanted someone to do a job for him. And for all she knew he was in cahoots with Nate and Sasha and would go running back and tell them about yet another failed venture from the girl who couldn't stick at anything.

Something pricked at the back of her eyes. She squeezed them closed. Oh, for goodness' sake, no tears.

When she opened them again he was still staring at her. Just staring, with a niggly frown dancing across his forehead.

After that outburst he was bound to go, but it felt strangely good to get it off her chest. Even to a grumpy stranger who clearly thought she was mad.

His head cocked to one side as he sat down again and indicated for her to do the same. 'You can't hire someone? A bookkeeper? An admin assistant?'

Besides the fact she had no desire to hand over her precious business management to someone else again, she had no cash for even part-time wages. 'Not unless I can pay them in doughnuts.'

'I hear they're considered legal tender in some parts of the world. Or at least they should be.'

He could joke too at a time like this? So maybe he was human after all. Surprising. Nice, actually. A glimpse of another side to him—something softer. Definitely more that she was intrigued by. Dammit.

She raised her glass to him and noted her hand was still trembling. 'Unfortunately, man cannot live by doughnuts alone.'

'No, I suppose not. But it would be interesting to try. For a day or two.' He picked up his glass and his hand brushed against hers. At the contact their eyes met for a beat, two. His gaze roved her face, her mouth, then dipped to her throat. Lower. And heat intensified in all the places he looked at. Unexpected. Inconvenient.

And something simmered there in his gaze too.

She pulled her hand away, reframing her thinking. She needed to get out of here quick sharp. She'd exposed her soul to him and now she was thinking strange thoughts. Was it hot out here? No, she was hot inside. 'So, take these menus to Lizzie. Show her. Discuss them with her. Tell her I'm more than happy to make other suggestions. I'd love to know what she thinks and to meet her, and the groom. Then, when you're done showing her, call me and we can talk further.'

'No.' He shook his head, his hand reaching out to her wrist, but she stepped back before he reached it. No more skin-on-skin action needed, thank you. 'I need to have this sorted. I'm away in Reykjavik next week, and after that it's getting far too close. I need certainties and decisions.'

'Well, like you, I have no time to waste and I am trying to be fair and honest with you.' Cassie sighed, projecting a calm that she didn't feel. 'She may insist she's going to do it herself; it may be her lifelong dream to do it—who knows? She's probably already started prepping and freezing things, then all this talk here with you is a complete waste of time.'

'Really? You think so?' He looked at her again and something zipped between them.

Under his searching gaze, Cassie felt like a rabbit caught in the headlights. For some reason his intensity slammed up against her resolve and threatened it. Luckily, Frankie arrived with the food. She hoped that would be enough to distract her from Jack Brennan's dark eyes and even darker voice—although she seriously doubted it.

CHAPTER THREE

So HE'D BEEN sucked in by a bleeding heart and a pretty face. Not for the first time and probably not the last.

No. Definitely the last. Jack didn't usually allow himself to be carried away by a sob story—unless it was for work, in which case it was the soppier the better; soppy made damned good TV. Soppy falling headlong into breakdown turned compelling into a road crash—the ratings always peaked. Great for his career, but out of bounds for his personal life.

But those big wide eyes and the crack in her voice had tugged at something deep inside him. He knew exactly what it was like to have someone steal his dreams. Time and again—and always just as he started believing they might finally come true.

So he'd stopped making dreams, simple as that. He'd clamped down on any kind of wishful hope that he was important enough for anyone to care about. Buried himself in study and work and stayed away from deep and dangerous, too burnt to foster anything more than a flimsy connection that he could break before someone else did.

But Cassie deserved a break. Right? And that was easy enough to do. So why did he feel as if he'd made a huge mistake just sitting here?

She looked a little nervous as she spoke between mouthfuls of the best taco shells he'd ever tasted.

Less hysterical, but nervous. 'Does your sister know about the car and the photographer?'

He wondered just how much more to tell her and decided to give her the basics. 'She wasn't going to have any frills. Friends are taking photos and she asked me to drive her to the venue in my car. She's a struggling artist marrying an equally struggling musician. They don't have cash to throw around; they can barely make the weekly rent. She's also a self-taught cook, and pretty bad, never having anyone to show her how to do these things growing up. But you try telling a woman that. Chances are she'll give everyone botulism.'

'I imagine the closest she'll get to hurting anyone would be killing you when she finds out about all this.' Cassie's brow furrowed into tiny lines. 'Provocation. Any jury would let her off.'

He ignored her little joke. 'Look, I want to give her the magical day she always talked about growing up—the whole meringue dress and rose petals shindig. But I'd like to get to the end of it without a trip to the emergency department or fending off an insurance claim.'

The frown deepened. 'Are you always this negative?'

Negative? Him? 'You don't know my sister. I prefer to see it as realistic. Plan for the worst, and so on.'

'And hope for what? The saying is: plan for the worst and hope for the best, right?' She pierced him with those eyes.

Hope that this marriage-fest would be over soon and he could get on with his life, guilt-free.

He watched Cassie take a long slow lick of a drip down the side of her hand and swallow the coriander and minty goodness. The way her tongue dipped across her suntanned flesh, the curl of a lock of hair framing her face, the light in her eyes as she caught him watching—a guilty twinkle. *God.*

His groin tightened.

Hope for what, indeed? A taste of her?

What? No way. No way. Na-ah. Pretty, yes. Attractive, even. But more than looking he couldn't—wouldn't—contemplate.

He ignored it. Tried to ignore it. Tried, too, to shake off the unnerving feeling that when she looked at him she saw a whole lot more than he wanted her to see.

Luckily, he was heading to Iceland tomorrow afternoon. The great thing about his job was that he was never anywhere for long. Guaranteed to stop any kind of meshing of minds. Meshing of bodies he could do—that didn't take too much investment. 'Hope that I can find a caterer who cuts me a bit of slack and stops talking in a foreign language about food stations.'

At this her eyes twinkled some more. 'My mum used to say that often things you're looking for are right in front of you. Which is usually the case for me—things I want are way too often in front of me, in a shop window display begging to be bought. Now, talking of mothers, what about the mother-of-the-bride? Is she likely to want to give her opinion too? Father?'

He felt his shoulders snap up at the mention of the woman who'd given birth to him and his sister, the blackness that filled that corner of his heart. She'd been no mother. Or the subsequent string of women who'd tried in vain to create the one thing he'd craved but had always had ripped away. Connection. Connection—like Lizzie was trying to create with Callum. He felt the blackness rise—that would mean putting his heart on the line again. No way. 'It's just the two of us.'

Pink patches took up residence on her cheeks, seeping down her neck in a rush. 'Oh. Okay. I'm sorry if I've overstepped—'

'Don't be. Now, are we done here?' He waved a pen-scribble action towards the door and a waiter nodded and disappeared for the bill. He needed space.

'I guess.' She looked a little put out at his brutal tone, and it might have been easy to clear the air—easy, maybe, for someone else. But hearts on sleeves was messy. Messy wasn't his thing.

While they waited for the bill he searched for something uncontroversial to cut through the heavy silence. Which was, after all, his fault. 'So what made you go into catering?'

'You mean my sister didn't give you the low-down of my life already?'

'Your sister's pretty protective where you're concerned.'

'She's lovely and everything, just sometimes a little stifling.' Fiddling with her bag, Cassie gave a gentle smile. 'Make that a lot stifling. Like you, maybe? With Lizzie?'

He felt the guilt shimmer through him. 'No. I don't stifle; it's hard to stifle when you're not even in the same country for most of the year. I'm always on the road shooting or editing. I'm not here enough, so she tells me. But I was asking about you and your career choice.'

Hell, he didn't need to have his relationships analysed. He knew he was bad at them. That was what this whole wedding food thing was about—making amends. Being the better guy. The better brother. Trying to create a happy medium between work and life. Instead of work and work...and work. Which until now had *been* his life.

Cassie shrugged her delicate shoulders as another curl fell from the chopsticks. And now his imagination ran riot with a few too many scenarios of that vivid red spilling over his bed, his back…

Whoa. Not a good idea.

She carried on chatting in her sing-song voice. 'Bottom line—I didn't know what I wanted to do when I left school so I dabbled in a few things, none of them particularly successful, but everything came back to how much I loved food. Eating, cooking, and I get a kick out of making food for other people to enjoy. My mum said it was my nurturing side. My sisters think it's all about the praise and attention. *Oh, such amazing flavours, Cassie…what adorable presentation, Cassie…you're so clever, Cassie…* And you've got to admit, you can't beat a bit of adulation, right? Mr Award-winning Film-man.'

'I'm more proud about the films than the awards. It's the craft I love, not the praise. The interesting and sometimes reluctant subjects…'

Her laugh rang through the evening air. 'My shy sister, a subject. She'd love that idea. Not. I can't believe you persuaded her to even be in one of your films.'

'It was for a good cause. They wanted to promote their charity work. Seemed a good trade-off for a fly-on-the-wall of their lives.'

In all his conversations with Sasha she'd missed out a lot of details. Like Cassie's hotness. Her irritating habit of telling people how to live their lives. Her scattiness. The humour. *The hotness.* 'She was definitely one of my more challenging interviewees. I had to work hard to get information out of her. But now I know a little about her life, about your dad.'

'Oh. Right. My dad? My dad.' Cassie swallowed her shock, but her eyes widened. 'You just come out and say it. Like that? Most people tiptoe…no, actually, most people don't mention it at all. Is that your media thing? Catch her off guard, throw in a curveball?' She looked over her shoulder. 'Are there hidden cameras?'

'Not at all.' He almost laughed at the thought. The stiffening of her back and the eye contact dodge wasn't lost on him, though; clearly, this was a subject she wasn't comfortable discussing. And who could blame her? He hadn't meant to stray into such difficult territory. And now he was here he didn't know how to reverse.

Her voice rose again. 'Wow. Well, that's another skeleton out of the cupboard then, but I think everyone knows that story now—it was front page for long enough. Your direct approach doesn't surprise me, though, Mr Brennan. Nor does it affect me—if that was your intention.'

Liar. She was a tight bundle of gelignite that looked about to explode at any moment.

Her father's betrayal by his business partner and subsequent suicide had been pretty high profile; it hadn't been hard for Jack to delve deeply enough to find that out. The effects on her family had been long-term and damaging. Not least that the Sweet sisters struggled to give trust easily—Sasha had been definitive about that.

So whatever had happened between Cassie and her ex business partner must have added deeply to her sense of mistrust. No wonder she was like a hot potato dancing in embers trying to make her business a success. She needed something to believe in. To make something hers. Just hers. 'I'm sorry, really. Wrong subject?'

'Understatement of the year. Seems we both have private things we don't like to discuss during a *business* meeting, Mr Brennan. I asked you about family because it was relevant. I'm not sure at all why you asked about mine. Now, where's that bill got to?' Scraping her chair back, she stood, shot him a wavering business smile and scooted to the door.

* * *

After a debate during which they agreed to split the bill—at her absolute insistence—Jack walked Cassie out on to the busy street. The bare skin on her arms shone in the street light. He'd never really noticed a woman's skin before, unless it was in front of his camera lens. Or the depth of blue in their eyes. Eyes that darkened to navy with anger, that glittered like a shimmering ocean when she laughed. And now he was thinking like a pathetic poet. While pure irritation shimmered through her.

'Do you want to get a cab, Cassie? I could drop you off.'

'No, thanks. I'll walk. Saves cash and the environment. Look, there's a taxi coming now—you want it?' She raised her hand to the oncoming black cab. It slowed towards them. 'I presume you'll call me when you've spoken to Lizzie?'

'Of course.' He'd been wrong about her. He'd thought the scattiness and the sensitivity were signs of weakness. But they were a sideshow. She had steel in that ramrod back and a streak of determination that bordered on reckless.

Nevertheless, he still seriously doubted she could pull off a decent wedding dinner without some sort of major mishap. The jury was still out on whether to take a risk and hire her.

Still, he wasn't prepared to allow her to walk the London streets on her own in the dark. She might not like it, but that wasn't under debate. He waved the cab on. 'Nah, it's okay. I'll walk too. You're on my way.'

'I'm further down Holland Park Avenue than you and then a little way off the main drag.'

'You're only a short detour.'

Her hand slipped to her hip. 'Seriously, I'm fine. I do this all the time.'

'Well, you shouldn't.' Could she not listen? He knew these streets. He would not let any woman walk home alone. He'd spent far too much time fighting for survival in the adjacent neighbourhood to know the dangers. 'It's not safe. I said I'll walk you.'

'Stifling much?' He didn't need to see her face to know she was rolling her eyes, and the thought of it amused him. 'It's fine, Mr Macho. I use knives for a living, remember? I know how to gut and bone and de-vein just about anything that moves. What'll you do?' Her eyes flicked to his jeans pocket. 'Wallet an attacker to death?'

'What do you know? I have black belt wallet ninja skills.' And a working knowledge of street fighting. Because he'd had to learn the hard way. Wrong kid, wrong street, wrong background. Every single time. Shifted from pillar to post. From house to house. His face had rarely fitted and he'd had to fight his way out of too many arguments.

But all she saw was a successful film-maker who had butted into his sister's wedding plans. Good. Because the less she knew about him the better. The past might have shaped him, but he didn't ever let it impinge on how he lived his life now.

At least that was what he told himself.

Cassie shrugged. 'Suit yourself. I don't need a bodyguard but keep up, I've got sums to do when I get home and I want a good sleep because I have an early meeting tomorrow. I don't have time to wait for stragglers.' Laughing, she wrapped a cream shawl around her shoulders and kept a brisk pace as they descended the hill towards Holland Park. This was no evening stroll for romantics. Not that he would ever use his name and the word *romantic* in the same breath.

He met her step for step. Too easy for a man who ran

marathons to keep flab and feelings at bay. 'So the personal chef gig—why did you choose that instead of opening your own place?'

'Are you still here?' She increased her pace past the still open shops and overflowing pubs. He wondered if she ever stopped. Just stopped. A fleeting image of her, slick and spent on his bed, flickered in his mind. Her eyes closed, body soft against his sheets, slow deep breathing. Relaxed. Still.

Sometimes being a film-maker played havoc with his sanity—he saw too many things in fast flickering images in his brain. Zooming in could be a pleasure and a curse. Right now, the latter.

She kept right on chattering, the tension from the café dissipated. Or it could have been that she was trying to keep him on side; it was no secret she needed his money, the job. So he supposedly had the upper hand. If only he could see it through the fog of chaos she created.

'This way I get to meet my clients in a more intimate environment, much preferable to working in a hot, noisy restaurant. Probably like you and your documentaries? You get the best out of people when there's less of a crowd, right?'

'And the worst. I didn't make a big splash on the documentary scene by finding the nicer parts of people's stories. Sadly, dirty laundry sells.'

'And there seems to be a lot around.' She nodded. 'Sometimes people plain forget that I'm there in their homes. You wouldn't believe some of the things I've seen and heard.'

'You want to bet? I've been on the road with rock stars. I reckon I can beat you hands down in the shock stakes.'

Slowing her pace, she looked at him, that teasing and

breathy voice becoming harder to ignore. 'Oh? Try me. A gory story smackdown. Excellent.'

Now this could get interesting. 'What does the winner get?'

She looked up at him for a few moments, blue eyes piercing, as if trying to read his mind. Oddly disconcerting. Because he could have sworn that she understood exactly what he was thinking. 'Winner gets...the satisfaction that they won?'

'I tell you, there is no competition. I'll win.'

'You like to win? You do seem the type.' Her mouth curled up at one corner. 'And you have that self-satisfied look already. How about this? Once I was serving dinner in a famous actor's house. But he was having it away with a guest upstairs, while his wife was downstairs tasting my crème brûlée.'

'Which actor?'

She tapped her nose. 'My secret. Confidentiality. I'm like a doctor with the Hippocratic Oath. Only not as clever. Or as...doctory.'

He couldn't help the laugh bubbling up from his chest. She was...well, she was just surprising. Warm and soft and smelling like a candy shop. 'Doctory? A technical term?'

'Obviously. My eldest sister, Suzy, is training to be a surgeon and she's very doctory. You know—bright and dedicated and compassionate.' They stopped at a crossing and waited for the red light, turned right past an old church on to tree-lined cobbled streets. One of the older and prettier parts of the area, a little more rundown than his mews, but nice enough. 'Okay. Your turn. Beat that.'

He sifted through the tales and memories of the last few years. Difficult to pick one that was funny and shocking but not too sordid. 'Threesomes, foursomes, wife-swaps. Drugs and alcohol. You name it, I've seen it or heard about it. But the strangest? I was once on tour with a band and the lead singer developed an explosive habit.'

'What do you mean? Drugs?'

'No. He blew up—literally detonated—something in every venue. Toilets, drum-kits, seats. He liked the poeticism of shards, apparently.' Jack shook his head. 'Okay, yes. Probably drugs.'

'Really? Blowing things up? Bizarre.'

'Win?'

'I don't know; I'm thinking. I must have something to beat that. Foursomes? Really? I don't even want to know how that works out.' Finally she came to a halt outside a row of neat terraced houses with window boxes that had brightly coloured plants trailing over them. A vivid splash in an otherwise unimaginative backdrop. Kind of like her.

She rooted in her satchel, tutted. Dropped it to the ground and spilled the contents out, handing bits of paper, a can opener, lipgloss to him as she searched, her fist getting lost amongst tissues and things he barely even recognised and surely should not be in a woman's bag. Was that a spanner? Eventually she pulled out a bunch of keys. 'Got them! Right. This is me. Number twelve. First floor. It's not much but it's home.'

These were renovated apartments in a decentish part of town. No wonder she was struggling to find the rent. 'You live here on your own?'

'Yep. It was always meant to be a work-from-home kind of thing with… Never mind.' Her shoulders hitched.

'Are you talking about paring knife man?' And why the hell he'd even asked and burst the first pleasant bubble of conversation they'd managed all evening, he didn't know. It was none of his business and in his haphazard personal life he always—*always*—stayed away from backstory. Unlike in his films, where he liked the present to be filled with regret and melodrama and lost chances. People searching for the whole happy-ever-after lie that littered cheap novels and rom-com films. The pursuit of all that filled his subjects with a hope that was rarely realised. Hell, it made addictive TV. Won awards.

She bit her bottom lip, then flashed him another of her smiles. This one was unconvincing. 'Okay, well, thanks for walking me back. I'll be fine from here. Have a safe walk home.'

'He broke your heart?' She'd already changed the subject but he wouldn't let her get away with it.

Cassie sighed as she shoved everything back into the Tardis-like bag. She blinked away a wisp of bitterness or sadness or just plain hurt and hid behind that enduring mask of cheerfulness. 'Absolutely not. He broke my bank balance and that's a whole bigger sin in my book. I'm over it and, make no mistake, I'm never going there again.'

He still wasn't convinced. 'You sure about that? What about the gooey-eyed romance thing? The wedding catering? Isn't it your job to believe in all of that?'

'For someone else, sure. My sister. Your sister. Everyone else. But not this sister.' Her finger pointed to her chest and he had no doubt that she believed it. Somewhere down the line she'd change her mind, but for now? He was willing to give her the benefit of the doubt.

The scent of her whirled around his head; the passionate tone to her voice, the fighting back, her chaos even, stoked something deep in him. The determined look in her eyes did nothing to dampen the fizz of something electric whizzing round his veins; if anything, it just made it stronger.

With a shock he realised he wanted to crush her against the wall and kiss her.

Turning to go up the steps, she waved. 'So call me when you've spoken to Lizzie and we'll sort out the menus.'

Like hell he was going to let her go that easily. 'And so now you're what? A nun? You don't do this ever?'

'Do what?' She paused.

'I want to claim my winner's prize.' Where in hell did that come from? He didn't know or care. The need to feel her mouth against his swelled inside him.

'What? We never agreed on a prize.' But the heat in her too-blue eyes told him she was just as interested as he was. If not for that he'd have walked right away. If not for that? And the fact she was a beautiful woman. And he was drawn to her in a way he hadn't been drawn to any woman in a long time. If ever. Which was why he should have taken her lead and walked away too. Put that sexy sway to the back of his mind, those pink lips, those dark navy eyes. The nagging feeling in his head that blared alarm bells.

Go home.

He made it up the first couple of steps towards her. At her frown he stopped short. Her mouth was inches away.

All he had to do was reach out.

'Jack.' It was meant to be a warning. A definitive *no*. But it sounded like a whimper. Worse, it sounded like an invitation. And maybe it was. Cassie didn't know. Didn't know anything really except that this man had stirred something in her that had long been dormant. Which was equal parts thrilling and scary. Actually, it was scary as hell.

Before she could breathe again Jack was in front of her, all six feet plus of impressiveness, his scent of heat and man filling her nostrils. His hard body…there. The open-necked shirt revealing just a little of a tanned chest that she suddenly wanted to touch, his smile finally now almost blossoming.

The street seemed to fade out a little as her vision narrowed to just him. His hand was on her cheek, the light-ness of his touch making her heart stutter. The intensity in his eyes causing her abdomen to contract with a need she hadn't expected.

This was utter madness. A choc chip short of a cookie. How could she want to slap him and kiss him at the same time? He was pompous and a giant pain in the ass yet she wanted to kiss him.

No. No. No.

Yes.

No. This couldn't be happening. But the more he looked at her, the more intense this urge to taste him grew.

'What's this?' His hand had moved across her cheek. She should have walked away, but that glittering in his eyes made her legs refuse to move.

She found her voice, but it wasn't her usual one. This was filled with desire, reedy, coarse. Husky. And speaking was difficult through a throat so dry and a mouth so wet. She ran a finger across her face and looked at the sparkles on her fingertips. 'It's gold dusting from the fairy castle. Wait, I'll just wipe it off. I can't believe I've been wearing it all evening and you didn't mention it.'

'Fairy dust? I like it. Let's just say for once I do believe in fairies. Even if they are a little on the manic side. And possibly crazy. And definitely disorganised.' His fingers closed around her hand and he pulled it away from her face. Then he stroked the glitter on her cheek.

Blood pounded in her ears. She opened her mouth to speak but he shook his head, his finger touching her lips and stoking that need with an extra helping of urgency. His delicious dark voice whispered along her neckline, 'I want to claim my prize and also win a bet with myself.'

'Oh? What's that?'

'That just for one second you will be still.'

He stepped closer and the scent of him caressed her, the sound of his ragged breathing stoked a fire in her belly. The heat in his eyes connected with something feral, something wild inside her. Her mouth watered at the thought of how he might taste. She put her hands out to keep a distance but her fingers curled into his shirt as if manipulated by some weird instinct that she just could not fight. 'I can do still.'

'Show me.' Then his tongue licked along her bottom lip—and heck if she wasn't frozen in place under his touch. Just the merest caress of his skin against hers had her anchored to the spot. All logic fled her brain and her body took over. Her eyes fluttered closed as that need swelled inside her. Hands held her shoulders as he dipped his head, his tongue moving over her mouth, gently teasing it open. Slowly. Achingly slowly. Every cell in her body jumped and danced but she didn't move, not one inch, save for a stuttering breath and a heart that threatened to pound out of her chest.

Then, unable to resist any longer, she opened her mouth to him. He tasted of danger. Intense, unfettered heart-pounding danger. And, as if that was all the encouragement she needed, she pressed against him, deepening the kiss, arms curling around his neck, breasts brushing against that hard wall of muscle. His hands cupped her face, his kiss urgent but soft, taking and giving. But it was far from sweet. It was rash, it was hot, it was everything she expected from him—and yet so much more. His tongue stroked against hers and deep in her gut she burnt bright white heat, her belly tightened.

This was purely physical. Nothing more. But for once it was so good to feel the warmth of strong arms holding her, making her believe that for a small selfish moment she didn't have to face everything on her own. Making her forget everything. Apart from this. Him.

His mouth traced a trail of kisses to her neck and she heard herself moan. Then he pulled her closer, groaning against her neck. The heat intensified to molten lava coursing through her body.

'Let's go upstairs,' he murmured.

Upstairs. The old Cassie would have jumped at the chance. She was on the verge of agreeing when cold reality slammed through her. She had to go upstairs to the flat she could barely afford and make her peace with her spreadsheet. She could not invite a man into her space to distract her from her goal. However good a kisser he was. However much her hormones rallied against her in some kind of sexual guerrilla warfare.

And then she was pulling away, her brain a muddled blur of wants and shoulds and reasons not to. That had been one hell of a mind-melding kiss. All rational thought had abandoned her. 'No. Look, I can't. I need to go. *Alone.*'

'Yes. Yes, of course.' And to be honest he looked a little unsettled too. Which gave her the tiniest amount of pleasure. Who'd have thought a kiss could rumple a man like Jack?

She sighed, rather too seductively for her liking because that was so not her intention. 'I promised myself I wouldn't do this. It's not the right time.' And if she was ever going to get involved with anyone in some parallel universe where she could actually trust a guy, it wouldn't be him. It would be someone who didn't do brackets, someone less bossy. Someone…her heart squeezed…no one.

'I'm not looking for forever.' The heat in his eyes began to dim. Fading. Fading…

She shrugged, wishing the light would dim inside her too, but it blazed too brightly. 'Me neither. But I'm also not looking for this.'

And the light was gone…over and out. Stepping back,

he shoved his hands in his pockets. 'You sure about that? A kiss? Some fun?'

'I'm sure. Totally sure. Definitely. Absolutely one hundred per cent sure.' Once again she was saying words and hoping that she'd damn well soon believe them. *Feel* them.

He stood, mouth half smiling, with a bewildered look in his eyes which made him even more attractive. How easy it would be to take a chance. To say: to hell with everything. To kiss that confused look into something hotter and sexier and satiated.

So tempting to drag him up to her flat by the lapels and forget about the promises she'd made.

But she turned and forced her feet up the pale stone steps, let herself into her apartment and steadfastly refused to look out of the window to see if he was still standing there. Part of her secretly hoping he was still there—and wishing him gone at the same time. Pouring herself three large fingers of cooking brandy, she took a long drink to try to erase the delicious taste of him. Swallowed a handful of chocolate-coated cherries. The last delicious red velvet cupcake. Feta cheese squashed onto a cracker. God, if she carried on like this she wouldn't fit into any of her clothes. Then she'd truly be the naked chef. Not a pretty prospect.

But it was no use. Jack was still there, with her, on her. There was no way she'd be able to make sense of those numbers on her spreadsheet now.

See? The infuriating man had messed up her timetable along with her resolve.

Looking around at her shabby but well-loved kitchen, she decided to do the only thing she knew that could relax her. So she set to work weighing and mixing, whisking egg whites and sugar and vanilla essence by hand until her arms hurt and she'd finally steadied her breathing. It took a while for her head to feel clearer and almost back to normal again as the scent of soft meringue cooking slowly in the oven filled the kitchen. But she knew it would take even longer to douse the heat zipping through her. She shouldn't have let him walk her home. Shouldn't have kissed him.

But she was glad she'd walked away and saved herself from the embarrassment of a one-night stand. Or the excitement of being with someone—with him—who knew how to do intense and even shyly funny and who was concerned about her safety and was sex on a stick. Who made her feel sensual and wanted and who was interested in her. Even if only for one night.

She was glad, wasn't she?

Truth was, after one bone-melting kiss with Jack Brennan she wasn't sure about anything any more.

CHAPTER FOUR

'I NEED TO talk to you, Lizzie. If you're there, pick up the phone. It's about the wedding. About the food... Hello? Pick up, Lizzie!' *Damn bad timing.* Jack batted his phone on the seat armrest just as the flight stewardess came over. She had a stern but interested glint in her heavily kohled eyes. Her hand ran down her thigh to straighten her skirt as she crouched next to him, picking up the empty glass of champagne and used hot hand towel.

God bless business class.

'Mr Brennan, we're taxiing to the runway; please switch your phone to the off position. Once we reach ten thousand feet you can use the Wi-Fi. But for now—'

'I know; I get it.' He clicked the phone off. At least he'd made good on his promise to Cassie—or tried to. But Lizzie kept irregular hours and once engrossed in her art she never even heard the phone ring. Now he was going to be stuck filming for a few days, then locked in an editing suite for the super-quick turnaround he'd promised. But he'd keep trying. This wasn't exactly the kind of thing he could leave a message about.

Hey, sis, I'm paying for the wedding food because you're a crap cook. Love, me.

Or, *Hey sis, I'm paying for the wedding food because I've been a crap brother. Love, me.*

There was a whole host of talking he'd need to do to explain that and his rush of guilt.

'My name's Estelle and if there's anything else I can help you with—anything at all—just press the call button.' The stewardess rested a manicured finger on the back of his hand and her eyelashes blinked rapidly. 'Anything.' The message wasn't lost on him.

Turning away, he shook his head. Nothing. He didn't want anything from her.

Which was strange in the extreme, because she was exactly the kind of woman he'd want things from, usually. Smart, independent, uncomplicated. *Serene*. Every step was controlled. Her facial muscles were tamed and unmoving. But that could have been the Botox. Her hands didn't gesticulate and fill the space as she spoke.

When he'd woken up that morning—after a strangely fitful sleep—he'd been unable to shed the feeling that kissing Cassie had been the dumbest thing he'd done in a while. And at the same time wanting to do it all over again. This time with a second course...and maybe more. Hell, she'd been the first thing he'd thought about as his alarm clock had blared, when most days he was filled with the rush of the day ahead, the love of his nomadic job—no two days the same.

Even the prospect of an exclusive interview with a famously reclusive star hadn't erased the image of her as she'd turned away. The questions and confusion in her eyes. Things he didn't know any answers to—and he shouldn't even try to find them.

So, as he was clearly under par, he wouldn't jump headlong into making a similar mistake again. Not with Estelle. And definitely not with Cassie.

He looked out of the window and watched London disappear below the clouds and with it he attempted to leave behind the events of last night. The soft touch of her lips against his. The little mewl of delight as she'd pulled him closer. The chaotic whirlwind she created wherever she went, including inside his head.

Especially inside his head.

He'd been torn between giving in to that sudden bolt of temptation or fighting it until he'd got her home safely. Because he got the impression that Cassie, with her muddle and fuss and her ardent words about his sister's special day, did believe in the hearts and flowers he so easily decried. So getting interesting in the sack with her would only lead to a bleeding heart, which he plain avoided at all costs.

He was not going to think about her. He was going to sit back, close his eyes and plan, frame by frame, his next assignment so that when he met with Andres, the sound engineer, he'd be one step ahead of the game. Jack prided himself on always being one step ahead of the game.

Unlike Cassie, who seemed to have life happen to her and dragged everyone else along for the ride. That wasn't what he'd worked so hard for. His childhood years had been chaos in the extreme and he never wanted to go back there again, to bewilderment and pain. No, he liked certainty and planning and order.

At that moment Estelle unclipped her seat belt and started to make her way over, determination lodged in that calm exterior. So she wouldn't disturb him he delved into his briefcase and pulled out a wad of paper. But when he looked down his stomach tightened. He'd lifted out the folder of Sweet Treats' menus and did he imagine just the faintest whiff of sugar?

Okay. So the fates were aligning against him. Typical. Just damned great. He hadn't even realised he'd put that folder in his bag. And so, it seemed, Cassie was playing games with his head even from hundreds of miles away.

Staring at the endless lists of food, he decided he might as well have some recommendations for Lizzie when he finally broached that thorny subject. Maybe if he presented her with such spectacular choices she'd be blindsided to his interference. Irritatingly, though, as he scanned the entrées, his attention was held not by the thought of smoked salmon and cream cheese blinis, but by the woman who was going to make them.

For once, Cassie was going to be on the other side of the serving hatch and she was determined to enjoy every single second. A sumptuous gala dinner, flowing wine and playing posh dress-up—what wasn't to like? As she adjusted the straps on her way too expensive but breathtakingly beautiful silver sparkly sandals, she glanced at the large clock above the ornate hotel door.

No. Really? Her stomach clenched. Did an hour past start-time count as fashionably late? No wonder there was no one around but doormen. One approached and asked for her ticket, which she handed over.

'This way, ma'am. Please be silent as we make our way through the ballroom. The awards have begun.'

'Sorry. Sorry. Sorry,' she whispered, as she followed the doorman's ramrod-straight back across the crowded dimly lit room to her allocated table, all the while trying to keep an eye on the stage, where someone was rambling about public service. Trying to gauge whether she'd missed her sister's award or not.

'Your seat, ma'am.' He pulled back a chair at a large round table set for dinner and she slid quietly into it, noticing that there were two empty seats facing her, where she assumed her sister and husband should be sitting. She nodded and smiled to the other guests at the table, apart from the man next to her—his body turned away from her, facing the stage, and way too familiar. She didn't need to see his face—every cell in her body jumped awake, knowing exactly who he was.

Jack Brennan.

No. A sense of dread danced with an eager bounce in her hormones as she took in the messy hair that was the only out-of-control thing in his whole demeanour. The stoic broad shoulders she'd leaned into, the back she'd run her fingers over, all dressed up in a suit that looked as if it came from Savile Row. Or wherever it was that fancy suits came from because, Lord knew, she'd only ever served people wearing them and had no clue where to buy them.

And now she was here next to him, the memory of that kiss manifested into two hot blotches on her cheeks—that were fast spreading into a full-blown rash on her chest. Great. She picked up the evening's programme and fanned herself with it. Was it necessary to have to carry ice cubes with her every time they shared the same air?

Note to self: enquire as to guest list for Sasha's future glitzy events.

She scanned around for another empty seat somewhere on another table—but there weren't any. Briefly considered crawling under the table and hiding out until he'd gone. But the dress was loaned and she really didn't want to ruin it.

She wasn't ready for this—to face him after that kiss—she'd planned on talking to him next week by phone—or preferably email. Then bypassing him altogether and going straight to Lizzie. And wasn't he meant to be somewhere very cold and far away? Although in reality he could have been in outer space and it wouldn't stop the memory of the heady rush of heat when his mouth had slanted across hers.

And wouldn't she know it, but being this close to him had her thinking about where else on her body his mouth could slant.

Stop that. She fanned the programme faster in front of her face—she couldn't think like that. Slanting was so off-limits.

She forced herself to focus on the speaker on stage but he came to an abrupt end and, as the rapturous applause finished, Jack turned to her. She didn't miss the quick dip of his eyes to his watch. 'Good evening, Cassie. Glad you could join us.'

Why the hell was he here? This was Sasha's night. Not his. An awards evening for her charity work. Why, oh, why had he suddenly become embroiled in her life? She put the programme down and fixed the best nonchalant smile she could muster, after re-clipping an annoying lock of hair that kept falling into her eyes. 'I know, I know. I'm late again. Don't look at me like that; I couldn't help it.'

'So what pressing culinary emergency happened this time? A cupcake crisis? Pancake pandemonium?' His suit jacket moulded around tight wide biceps as he leaned forward. The crisp white shirt and dark blue tie gave him an air of sophistication that made her breathless and hot. The world tipped a little as he nodded. He seemed to think, underneath that grumpy irritated exterior, that this scenario was mildly funny.

'If you must know, I was completing my end-of-year accounts and I got to a tricky bit. Well, a few tricky bits.' It was all so tricky—none of it made palatable reading. And it had taken her a lot longer than she'd planned. Boy, she wished she'd paid attention at school instead of playing hooky with her friends.

And, even more, she wished she was in a better financial situation to be able to tell Jack Brennan what he could do with his wedding breakfast, if for nothing else than to preserve her sanity and try to erase the memory of those lips on hers. *Go, and be damned, Mr Brennan.* But now she'd confirmed she really, really needed his money. Swiping her hands together, she gave him a self-satisfied grin. 'Done. Finished. *Finito*.'

His eyebrows rose—impressed or disappointed? She couldn't tell which. 'In August? Aren't they due in October?'

'Apparently so. So whoop-de-do me. Yay.' She gave a small fist-pump but didn't think it prudent to mention they were last year's accounts, so already ten months late. Mr Frumpy Grumpy would scowl even more. In fact, until she'd received the final notice and threat of legal action that morning, she'd put the whole tax thing to the bottom of her list. But heck, it had been swiftly moved up. And now she'd finished them and sent them and felt, for the first time in a few weeks, a little lighter. So she'd come out hoping to relax and he was going to spoil that. Because how could she relax with that kiss hovering between them? 'Shouldn't you be in Iceland?'

'It was only a four-day job. Got back this afternoon, just in time for this. Nate invited me ages ago and I didn't want to miss it. Between them, your sister and her husband have raised a lot of cash for special needs kids.'

'Well, lucky me.' Glancing at the empty seats, she felt a twinge in her heart. 'Have I missed them? Please don't tell me I'm too late to cheer her on. This means so much to her.'

'So you could try using a watch?'

She tried to stop her shoulders from slumping, not least because her dress was so low-cut she was in danger of spilling her assets on to her side plate. 'I don't need a watch; I just need more time in the day.'

The frost seemed to melt a little. 'You look very different tonight.'

Was it because his eyes had followed the line of her cowl neckline? And he liked what he saw. Clearly. If only

there'd been any possible way she could have worn a bra—
but backless was backless. The edges of his mouth tilted
upwards as she sat up straighter and patted the soft folds
of black chiffon fabric against her chest, then made sure
the shoestring straps were in place, holding the whole
thing together. Tying the damned things at the small of
her back had been a feat even a contortionist would have
struggled with.

'Thank you.' She caught herself staring into those dark
eyes for way longer than she should.

He shook his head as if he couldn't make any sense of it.
'Sasha and Nate have been backstage most of the evening;
Nate did a song and handed out a few awards. If you take
the time to read the programme instead of whipping up a
whirlwind with it, you'll see they're up next.'

'Oh, good. I'm so glad. I didn't want to let her down.'

'Don't worry. They don't know you were late. Relax,
Cassandra.' No one ever called her that. No one. It had
been something teachers used whenever she was in trouble.
But heck, listening to that voice whisper her name, feeling the strange tumbling in her stomach and hot points of
raw need in inconvenient places—she was in trouble all
right. Big trouble. He poured a large glass of champagne
and handed it to her. 'You did miss dinner, though, but it
can be our secret. I won't tell if you don't.'

She took the glass from him and had a sip, tried to concentrate on the tickle of bubbles down her throat rather
than the tickle of butterflies stretching their wings in her
stomach just from being next to him.

This was ridiculous. He was a client. She'd dealt with
lots of clients before and none had made her tickly inside.
'I don't want to share secrets with you, Jack Brennan.'

'Are you sure about that?' The intense stare was mock-
ing and teasing. Serious—yet there was a glimmer of

amusement. Once again she got the feeling he was holding back every ounce of emotion, be it humour, anger or desire. The man was the very essence of self-control.

And she was torn between shaking him and kissing him again. Just for a reaction. Something unprepared, spontaneous. Just to see those gilded sparks in his eyes again. The ones he'd had trouble hiding last week. Would the real Jack Brennan please stand up? 'Yes. Absolutely. No secret-sharing.'

'Because if you're talking about the other night…?'

She held up a finger. 'No. Don't talk about it. Pretend it never happened.'

'What never happened?' He was closer now, his musky male scent joining in the teasing, adding yet another thing she had to try to ignore.

'The kiss.' Even as she said it her eyes drifted to that sensual mouth, her body burning with a need for more. But she dampened it down. She would *not* kiss him again.

His stare deepened, glittering. *Gotcha.* 'What kiss?'

'Atta boy. You really aren't just a pretty face.'

'Apparently not.' He clinked his glass against hers and took another drink. 'But, just for the record, you do taste good.'

Whoa. When he allowed himself to let go a little he certainly left an impression; this time it was heat seeping across her abdomen. 'Okaaaay. What did we have for dinner? In case she asks.'

'It was chicken stuffed with cheese. Some potato and cream thing and boiled vegetables. Nice.'

She laughed. 'Have you ever thought of becoming a food critic? Or making some kind of reality food programme?'

'No?'

'Good. Don't. The way you describe any kind of edible dish is an insult.'

'Food is food, however you dress it up.' His voice whispered over her neck like a soft summer breeze, sending ripples of desire skittering through her.

'Don't tell the Michelin chefs that or you'll be banned for life.'

'With their reduction of *jus* of lamb's lettuce on a deconstructed vol-au-vent? That kind of talk is just food porn.'

'No.' But with that voice saying those words it was a close run thing—making the food sound impossibly sexy. She imagined him feeding it to her with his fingers.

She really was losing her mind.

A hush rippled through the room, a clinking of knives against glassware as the MC entered the stage. His words of praise for her sister's charity work brought a tear to Cassie's eye. Sasha had fought hard to find her happy ending—and had made a lot of other people happy along the way—even if her Mr Right hadn't turned out to be the kind of guy she'd planned for. But then Sasha had always believed the right guy would be out there somewhere. Unfortunately, Cassie didn't share her sister's optimism.

After the award-giving and speeches a waiter arrived and served them with chocolate mousse. Cassie blew the errant curl of hair from in front of her eyes again and was just about to dig in to the dessert when Jack's hand was on her wrist.

'Your hair. Wait.' Reaching up, he softly took the curl, twirled it a couple of times through his fingers then clipped it into place on the side of her head. 'There you go. Shouldn't get in the way now.'

A shiver of goose bumps ran the length of her body. 'Thanks. You seem pretty adept at doing that.'

'I used to do my sister's hair when she was little.'

'Oh. That's…' Cassie's chest tightened. It had been such a tender and innocent gesture and an even more honest and sweet admission that she could feel her defences stripping away. And even though she knew it would be stupid to find out anything more personal about him, she couldn't help asking, 'That's an odd thing for a brother to do. Why you? Why did you do it?'

He looked away, as if deciding what to say. When he turned back to her, his face was serious. And she recognised the one thing she knew about Jack Brennan by now—he was hiding something. Something that hurt deeply. 'Shh. I think someone's about to say something on stage.'

Another tinkle of knives on glasses and more awards were announced. For a few moments she couldn't help but watch him out of the corner of her eye. The proud, successful media man with a string of his own awards. Who had tidied his sister's hair. Who was hell-bent on organsing her wedding yet woefully reluctant to share anything deeper than a paper cut. Every time she thought she was digging deeper he slammed a wall up.

And he was the wiser one here. Because she didn't need to know more, didn't need to know a great deal about him past his choice of lemon or hazelnut chocolate torte.

She'd make a point to ask him whether he'd spoken to Lizzie about the wedding just as soon as it was appropriate, to make an appointment to see her and get this wedding over with. That was, after all, the only thing she should be interested in.

Jack was hanging on with white knuckles. Four days in the freezing Arctic Circle had had absolutely no effect. He was still hot as hell for Cassie. He managed to keep his libido almost in check until the awards ceremony ended and the dance music began. Within seconds, Nate and Sasha had appeared on the dance floor and he watched Cassie watching them.

If he'd thought rationally he'd have known she'd be here tonight. But rationality had fled somewhere around the moment he'd taken those steps towards her outside her apartment, and had been strangely elusive ever since.

And if he'd thought she couldn't be any more attractive than wearing a flimsy gypsy get-up he'd been woefully wrong on that account too. Because here she stood out as the most beautiful woman in the room. Apart from that cute strand that kept bobbing around her cheek, her hair was swept up in a neat sophisticated style, showing off her delicate cheekbones and long graceful neck. But the dress. Man. Barely-there soft black fabric that hugged her curves, falling to layers and layers of skirt. He ached to run his hand around that nipped-in waist.

And the back. Whoa. He swallowed. Hard. His fingers itched to untie the tiny ribbons that criss-crossed her smooth straight back and let that delicate fabric fall to the floor.

Even though his wayward hormones had reached fever-pitch he was sitting here almost bleating on about a past he'd buried. Something he never did. Because he'd spent many, many years avoiding any kind of emotional connection—and there was something about Cassie that seemed to be hammering on that barricade just a little too loudly.

Beautiful, yes. Sensual, yes. But wild and unleashed, untamed. There was too much risk with this woman. She knocked him off his guard, made him say things that should never be said; either flirty and funny—which he just wasn't used to doing. Or deep and meaningful, which was worse. She had too much of an effect on him. Too much.

He needed to leave. On his own. To pass Cassie's details over to his sister and have nothing more to do with her. But there was Nate, nodding and gesturing for them to go join them on the dance floor. He was here by Nate's invitation—it would be rude to not take an interest in his family. Even though dancing and he were very rare bedfellows. Watching, yes. Moving, no.

He caught her attention. 'That dress was made for dancing.'

She shook her head and ignored his outstretched hand. 'Yes, but unfortunately this body isn't, plus I need to go home. Now.'

That body was made for kissing. For his hands. For his bed. For someone who wasn't so damned buttoned up. For someone, not him, who was willing to take a risk. Could he? The notion flitted through his head. 'You don't dance? Every woman likes to dance, surely?'

'Oh, don't get me wrong. I love to dance.' She laughed, pressing a napkin to her lips and smudging red lipstick a little onto the side of her mouth. 'Or what could loosely be described as dancing. Let's just say my admin skills are better than my co-ordination. But I can't.' She pouted. 'No play time for me and, believe me, that is a hard slap of reality for the number one party girl. How life changes.'

He imagined her in full good-time throttle and the thought of her bright light partying hard almost blinded him. Offering his hand again, he nodded to it. 'Come on then, just one dance—help me out here. Nate and Sasha are waving us over. Don't leave me standing here like a lemon.'

'No. I really do have to go. I've got to prep for tomorrow.' She stifled a yawn and for the first time he noticed dark circles under her eyes. Fatigue laced her voice and he felt a pang of guilt that he'd berated her for being late. It wasn't as if she was putting her work second to a hedonistic lifestyle. 'It's a corporate buffet lunch. I should have done it earlier, but there was the tax thing and then I needed to come here so I have a lot to do when I get home.' She waved at Sasha and stood, picking up a jewelled clutch bag and shoving it purposefully under her arm. 'This party is well and truly over for me. Enjoy the rest of the night. Ciao.'

And with that she turned her back. Giving him the glorious view of a sharp, elegant backbone, of ribbons that begged to be undone and a distinctly disturbing feeling that things were far from over.

CHAPTER FIVE

An hour later, with fifty bread tartlet shells cooling on a rack, lamb meatballs rolled and resting and hummus whizzed to within an inch of its life, Cassie leaned against her kitchen bench and took a long, slow breath. Damn the man. Even heavy-duty cooking hadn't been able to save her from her thoughts. It would have been very easy to slip into those arms, to feel the strength emanating from him. To rest her head against that crisp shirt. To breathe in that male smell. Too easy.

But she'd scraped together every scrap of self-control and left.

Yay, me.

Jeez, self-control was a real doozie. She still wanted his hands on her. To taste him again. But wanting and having weren't part of her plan. Her business was. Strictly business. And, by the look of her to-do list, the business would be keeping her up into the small hours tonight.

She hauled a large bag of kiwi fruit from her pantry cupboard and began to peel, jumping when her front door buzzer blared through her daydreams.

She pressed on the intercom button. 'Hello?'

'Hey, Cassie.' The voice was unmistakable. Her heart skittered and jumped, despite the knowledge that having him distract her again would probably mean working through the night. All she needed was dreamboat man in her house and her self-control would spoil like over-microwaved chocolate. A sticky, unusable mess.

'Jack? What do you want? It's late. I'm busy.' Her own voice was thready and high, yet hoarse. She leaned her head against the wall. *Lead me not into temptation.*

'You forgot something.'

'Oh? Okay, thanks. I'll come down.' When she opened the door he was standing half sheltered by her first-floor balcony, rain falling in thick sheets onto the rest of him. His penguin suit thoroughly and totally soaked, no tie, his open-necked shirt sticking to him, hair slicked across his forehead. But his eyes were lit with a bright heat.

His expression was dark and intense. 'You got changed. Pity.'

Whoa. That was unexpected. The man was usually so uptight. Now he was here, saying things that made her hot and jittery.

'Cooking's hard in a cocktail dress. Those domestic goddess types don't really exist, you know. Don't believe everything you see on the television. You, of all people, should know that.' Although she wished she hadn't chosen her slouchy yoga pants and a washed-out singlet topped off nicely with a sexy devil apron. She watched his gaze travel down her front to the slogan: *Too Hot to Handle*, the cartoon picture of a semi-naked hot body clad in tight red bikini, large comedy boobs and forked tail. And winced. Always the dream was better than reality, in so many ways. 'It was a gift.'

'Very thoughtful. Very interesting. And are you? Too hot?'

Looking at him? She couldn't be any hotter. 'Just fine, thanks.' Confused, she noted his empty hands. She had her bag and her shoes—that was everything she'd taken out with her for the evening. Through that strange hoarse voice that was thick with want she spluttered, 'So, what did I forget?'

'This.' Without any hesitation, he stepped into the hall-way, hands circling her waist as he crushed his mouth onto hers, filling her with his taste. There was no time to re-sist—not that she could have if she'd wanted to. This time he branded her with his mouth-scorching kisses across her lips, her neck. There was nothing tender or gentle. His face was intense, shadowed, his smell of elemental man and heat firing all her senses.

Breath stalled in her chest. He was here. For her. Taking what she'd tried so hard not to give. But how could she re-sist this? Him? She'd pushed him away earlier; she sure as hell didn't possess enough restraint to do it a second time. Snaking her hands around his neck, she pulled him closer.

'God, Cassie.' His mouth was close to her ear, his voice a wicked whisper that somehow hit every hot spot between her head and her toes. 'Still no bra?'

'You noticed?'

'You're joking? Every guy in the room noticed. Every guy watched you. Every guy wanted you.' For a man usu-ally so controlled there was nothing in his demeanour that showed turning up wet and uninvited was stepping out of his comfort zone. That saying words that made her belly fizz was in any way unusual. Every step was measured, intent. And hot. So hot. Was this a glimpse of the real Jack? If so, he was mind-blowingly sexy.

When his hand reached under her top and his palm closed over her breast, a moan escaped her lips—an au-tomatic instinctive reaction that she couldn't control. Her thoughts became wisps of nothing against the sexual need that swelled within her. Her body overrode any rational notion. She pressed against him, closing off any space be-

tween them, greedy for more of his touch, her hands flat
against a body that she was sure would look a heap better
without those wet clothes slicking to it.

His hands trailed from her breasts, leaving them aching
for more of his touch, to her bottom, and he lifted her from
the floor. 'Cassie, no underwear at all? Really?'

'Really. It's a comfort thing.'

'It's a turn-on thing,' he growled as he pressed even
closer, hands closing over her bottom, edging closer and
closer to the inside of her thigh.

Thanking the god of body control knickers that she'd
had the foresight to take them off—rather, squeeze them
off before they severed her circulation—she curled her legs
round his waist, felt the hardness of his erection tease her
sweet spot. Pinning her against the wall, he deepened the
kiss. Her hands shook as she gripped his shoulders then
explored the taut outline of his back, his throat, his hair.
She eyed the stairwell and wondered briefly whether her
neighbours might appear at any moment. But she almost
didn't care. She gave in, instead, to the pleasure of his
tongue on her skin.

How long he kissed her she didn't know but when he finally pulled away she felt bereft. Lost. Desperate for more.

Her mouth tingled with the pressure from his. The
mouth she wanted to feel in other places too. She thought
he was going to do more. To offer her more. She wanted
more. 'Well, wow. That was…something else.'

Resting his forehead against hers, he bridled his rapid
breathing. 'What was?'

'That kiss.'

'What kiss?' He gave her a reluctant smile, playing her
as she'd played him earlier. Ha, as if she could pretend
that kiss had never happened. Twice. Instead of giving
her more, he shrugged and lowered her to the floor. The

places his hands had been literally begged to be touched and stroked again. But he was clearly reining in his desire. 'So how's the prepping going?'

He wanted to talk about work? After that? Work could go to hell. She wanted to lock lips with him again and again until she'd had enough. Would that ever happen? He stood straight and brushed her hair from her face, his eyes serious and...concerned? Which was a little freaky because she'd have bet anything that concern was not what he wanted to convey.

'The corporate lunch?' Yes, he wanted to talk about her work.

And, really, work couldn't go to hell. 'I'm getting there. A couple more hours and I'll be done.'

If she wasn't mistaken, he was working through something in his head. He looked conflicted and immediately regretful of the kiss, but he gestured upstairs. 'Then what are we waiting for? I'm here to help.'

Oh, she had a list of things he could help her with and none of them involved food. Actually, visions of the man butt-naked apart from a few strategically placed strawberries and an indecent amount of whipped cream tripped through her brain. That could be fun.

No.

She took a long look at him, wondering if he was the kind of man who would let loose in the bedroom. Hell, he'd surprised her by just turning up uninvited. And she really knew she should just make him go and let her get on with her work—if not for the list of reasons that had earlier been playing round and round her head like catchy tasteless elevator music. *Numero uno* being the fact that the last time she'd let a man into her home he'd disappeared with the contents of her bank account.

But, truth be told, she had an unfathomable amount

of chopping to do. If she made sure she was in charge and didn't let herself get carried away by looking at him, things would be okay. Just once. 'Well, okay, but don't touch anything unless I tell you. And be careful with the knives; they're sharp.'

'Not a patch on your smart tongue, I'm sure. And thanks always goes down well.'

'Thanks. I mean it, really. Thank you for coming round.' And for the kiss. *Kisses*. Hot damn, she was supposed to be avoiding more contact, not encouraging it.

'My pleasure. But that...' he pointed to the wall he'd pressed her against and for a moment she thought he might do it again, but his jaw clenched just a little and she got the impression his resolve was a lot stronger than hers when it needed to be '...that had better not happen again. I will help you work, then I'll leave. You do not want to get involved with me.'

'Who said involved?' Strawberries and cream sounded just about right—a light snack, delicious and indulgent and with only a very short season. She had to admit the thought was very appealing.

But he was right. She bumped back down to earth. A light snack never quite sated her appetite and always left her wanting more. Seemed her judgement went awry the second he was in the vicinity. 'Don't worry. Didn't I already say I wasn't looking for anything? I'm not that kind of girl.'

'Good.' He looked satisfied with her answer, but not necessarily convinced. 'I don't want either of us to get the wrong idea.'

'No wrong idea here. A kiss doesn't mean anything.' She'd had lots of kisses before. Although none had affected her quite like his had. It felt as if there was something there between them—almost tangible. A something that could expand and become deeper. Something real.

His voice lowered. 'That didn't mean anything? Really? If you say so, Cassie. But it is not happening again. Okay?'

He ran his thumb over her bottom lip and the shock of his touch rippled through her again. That was real. Her response to him was real. The way he could see through her, into her, see what she needed and then provide it was real.

It meant something.

That was the problem. His problem.

Fear slammed through her. He was right. There was something here that neither of them wanted. Needed.

Real and downright terrifying. 'Okay. I hear you.'

His hand was reaching to the door. 'Look, maybe this was a stupid idea. I'll go. I'm sorry. Really, I shouldn't have come.'

'So why did you?'

Instead of twisting the doorknob, he raked his hand across the back of his neck. 'Ah, I don't know—you looked like you needed some help so I took a risk.'

That would have been big for him. He'd taken a risk on kissing her too and now neither of them knew what to do. Because it would be a bigger risk to take things to the next level and that was something neither of them wanted. She needed another relationship disaster like she needed a hole in the head. And Jack had *no commitment* written all over him. He didn't need a sign on his forehead; it was just there in his eyes.

So he regretted it already. Rash and hot and stupid. All the things she had definitely not put on her to-do list.

What she did know was that if she didn't make something good between them now then the next time she saw him it would be too embarrassing, too mortifying. He might even decide things were too difficult and not use her catering services. So she couldn't afford not to keep him on side. She just had to stop kissing him.

Trying to lighten the mood, she kept the tone casual. 'Okay, well, if you've come all this way to be my kitchen slave I've got four dozen fruit kebabs spoiling upstairs while we dither about here. Are you going to help me or not?'

'Are you sure?' He huffed out a long breath and seemed relieved that things were getting back to a non-kissing controlled normal.

'Yes. Absolutely, because now you owe me. Time is money, you know, and I can't waste it deliberating with you. We have work to do.' Turning her back, she put a foot on the bottom stair, wondering if she turned round again she'd see the door closing and him gone. 'Last one upstairs does the washing-up. And, believe me, I've used every darned pot in the house.'

'Okay. You're on. But you have to know, I run marathons just for fun.'

That explained the exquisite musculature she'd felt as she'd straddled him. *God.* She didn't know if her woeful self-control could last an hour. 'No one runs marathons for fun. We'll go on my count of three. One, two...' And she was off, leaving his laughter and calls of 'cheat' behind her.

No doubt Mr Fabulous lived in an expensive house with beautiful things—his address certainly screamed *desirable*—but hers was more comfortable. Okay, shabby, with its mismatched and borrowed furniture. Nevertheless, she loved her apartment, its location and potential, and had filled it with the most vibrant things she could find. Things that made her happy. Interesting things that made her smile. Although, looking at it through Jack's eyes, she thought maybe she'd gone a little too rainbow and not enough beige.

No. There was never a call for beige.

Jack shielded his eyes as he peered into the lounge. 'Whoa. Have you got a pair of shades I could borrow?'

'It has life. Energy. And I love it.' She picked up a bright turquoise shawl she used as a throw and folded it along the arm of her plaid sofa. 'Everything in here has a story attached to it. I had grand plans to do the interior design thing but I'm focusing my money in another direction.' Decorating and furnishings had gone down the same gurgler as financial security the day he who shall not be named had left town. And if that wasn't a salient enough reminder not to get involved she didn't know what was. The faint tinge of the battles she'd fought ever since coated her words. But she was winning them. Slowly but surely. 'So I had to buy furniture from the market or second-hand shops. But you can get some really fun things from there.'

'I said it was bright; I didn't say I don't like it. It has character. But then I wouldn't expect anything less coming from you.'

'It's not to everyone's taste.'

'There's taste here? Where, exactly?' Picking up a giant stuffed patchwork hippopotamus with a missing ear, he shook his head. Then he held her gaze for a moment as he smiled. And it almost took her breath away. There were glimpses of a kind man. One who held himself aloof, tried not to give too much away, tried to hide how his past had made him so cautious. But, just every now and then, that mask slipped, allowing her to see the man underneath. Kind, cautiously funny. Beautiful. He turned towards the kitchen, eyed up the sack of fruit and shrugged off his jacket. 'Right. What needs doing?'

'You really can cook? I thought you said—'

'No, I haven't a clue, but I can chop things. Surely it's not that hard?'

'Sure. No reason for catering college at all. Anyone can do it. Obviously, Jamie, Gordon and Nigella all found worldwide success with just a bit of random chopping and uncomplicated slicing.' Stabbing him with a skewer would possibly be petty considering his talent for kisses and his offer of help. 'Really? It's disappointing to have to add you to the list of people who don't take me seriously. Damn it, Jack—it's an art form. You know, like your job? Or is film school overrated too? Anyone can point a video camera and shoot these days, right?'

He held his hands up in submission and laughed. 'Okay. Sorry. You've got that paring knife locked away?' His shoulders lifted. 'Perhaps I can just peel something?'

'Do not touch anything. I'll show you what to do, but first I'll grab you an apron—oh.' She was enjoying bossing him around until she noticed his lips were a faint tinge of blue. 'You're dripping all over the floor—you must be freezing. God, you'll get pneumonia. Wait—I'll go have a look for something dry you can put on.'

'I'll be fine. Seriously, don't fuss. If you have a towel, that'll be great.'

'You'll drip onto the kebabs. No way. That has to be a health and safety issue. Take your clothes off and I'll put them in the tumble dryer.'

His eyebrows rose as he laughed again. Deep and long and just…lovely. His eyes crinkled and his smile was fresh and free. How a man could look so breathtaking just by being momentarily happy she didn't know. But it was a rare thing to see him relax. Intense was great and that fired a passion in her too, but relaxed and free was better. Such a shame they had a kissing embargo because that mouth looked ripe for it.

'Seriously? You're ordering me to get undressed? Is this what kitchen slaves have to do?' he asked.

Yes, please. 'Well, no. Not in here. In the bathroom. Or something.'

He glanced down at his long, long legs. 'And you have clothes to fit me?'

'I don't know. I'll find something.' Actually, she really didn't know. She didn't have any men's clothes, having set fire to the few things Patrick had left when he'd stayed over with her kitchen blowtorch. But it didn't matter—the guy was wet and he needed to take those clothes off and quickly. Slipping into her bedroom, she closed the door and leaned against it, trying to stop her hands from shaking, squeezed her body into a tight knot of restrained excitement and inhaled sharply. Fist pumping the air, she allowed herself a little crazy dance. So, okay, they'd sworn off kissing. But hell, he was here. He wanted to help. And very soon he would be naked.

Left alone with nothing but a whiff of a sweet smell that fired directly to his groin, Jack looked around the dazzling yellow kitchen, at the neat rows of tiny tart cases and clingfilm-wrapped meatballs on the bench top. At the alphabetised spices, the lists of food ticked off in neat cursive handwriting.

He thought about her impassioned rant and realised he had seriously misjudged Cassie. Yes, she was a flake when it came to organising her life—she was loud and messy and habitually late, but she knew her stuff and took her job very seriously.

And her skin felt like silk that he wanted to run his fingers over again. Her breasts were just perfect, responsive to his touch, firm yet soft. Her mouth was funny and haughty and sassy—and downright X-rated. And she had no underwear on. Commando. Naked. Under that ridiculous apron. That she even owned something like that made him smile—made her more fascinating. That she wandered through her apartment with no underwear on made her much more interesting indeed.

That kiss had been the far side of stupid. A wicked way of trying to get her out of his system that had spectacularly backfired. Need for the woman ran through his veins.

It had taken every bit of willpower he possessed not to undress her there in the stairwell, but it wasn't the way she looked that held him in thrall. Sure, she was beautiful, but there was so much more to her. A fight, a spirit, her sense of humour. A package that would keep him interested well beyond sex.

He was way out of his depth. This whole wedding breakfast escapade had thrust him into scenarios he hated and usually avoided at all cost. Tomorrow, he would be pitted against his sister, discussing her disastrous cooking which, in comparison with spending a few hours here not touching Cassie, would be a relative walk in the park. What the hell had propelled him over to her apartment in the middle of a rainstorm, he didn't know. But he couldn't sleep without kissing her again. She had a strange hold over him—too intense too quickly. So he figured it'd burn out pretty much as quickly as it had started.

He hoped it would because he was damned sure he didn't want to live like this—thinking about her, wanting her. He'd come here because he'd had an unshakeable feeling that she needed help. An irresistible feeling that they hadn't finished what they'd started—either by conversation, or by touch. And, yeah, he'd come here to kiss her again. *Dammit,* the woman was making him feel things. He didn't want that—didn't want a connection that would make him raw and exposed—he knew too well how destructive that could be. Glancing at the front door, he wondered whether he should just make an exit while she was out of sight. Leave a note. Send a text. Find another caterer.

'Here we go.' Too late. She bustled back into the room. It seemed Cassie rarely did anything sedately. Bustling, rushing, gesticulating. Thrusting a white chef's top and blue-check trousers into his fist, she smiled, a little bashful. The dance they were doing around each other now was laden with that kiss. And the struggle against more. 'I hope they fit. I'd forgotten I had them. They belonged to my catering tutor and he left them here.'

'Oh? Tell me more. He left them in your bedroom?' And why the desperate feral reaction in his gut at the thought of her with another man? It fuelled his desire to have her now. To make her his. Overrode any rationality.

He put the clothes on to the bench top, shrugged off his damp jacket and started to unbutton his shirt.

Her eyes followed the movement of his fingers as he popped each tiny pearl, the stuffy, humid late summer air in the tiny room becoming thicker and electric. 'Oh. Well...I had a party ages ago. He spilled...'

Her throat moved up and down as she swallowed. She wanted him, regardless of their agreement. Her cheeks blazed almost as bright as the hair that she'd scraped into a scruffy ponytail. And, despite her less elegant choice of clothes—the woman would look amazing in a potato sack—she emanated pure sensuality. Her lips still glistened with a sparkling gloss, but her eyes were heavy with unadulterated desire. And there was nothing more of a turn-on than knowing a beautiful woman wanted you— so much so her speech was befuddled. 'Some...tomato... Where was I? What?'

Watching her tongue-tied reaction made him hard. Intensely hard. 'Spilling something. So you didn't sleep with your tutor, then?'

'What? Gay Gareth? No way.' Her tongue darted out as she moistened her bottom lip, her hand lifted halfway between them—as if she was subconsciously reaching out to him. 'Hilarious. No. Just a major food-processing accident with tomato juice. It almost redecorated the kitchen too. Not pretty.'

Her eyes didn't stray from his chest. Tension vibrated through the room, sucking the oxygen out, thick and warm. He'd just stated his mission to help and then go home. She'd agreed. Hell, he'd even taken a step towards the front door.

His heart thumped loud and hard against his ribcage as he gauged his next move. Hers. But he didn't want to stop. Didn't want to see the heat in her eyes diminish. Didn't want to chop or slice. She turned away but he caught a glimpse of her fisted hands and a frisson of anxiety flitter across her eyes. 'This is so unfair. Either leave now or go and get changed. Out of here.'

'Right. Bathroom. I'll just be a minute.' He stifled a grin, grabbed the pile of clothes and headed to the cluttered bathroom. Worse still to be in her private space, where her smell intensified and everywhere he looked he imagined her. In the shower. Wearing the ridiculous duck shower cap. Luxuriating in the pink bath foam. Wrapping her naked body in the bright citrus-coloured towels.

Twisting on the tap, he stuck his head under and wondered just how much dousing in cold water he needed to be able to get rid of the heat suffusing him right now.

CHAPTER SIX

'So this is what we do; thread a piece of each of the fruit onto these wooden skewers. Grape first, strawberry, melon, pineapple and kiwi. Easy. Make it neat. Every skewer has to be as uniform as the others. That's it.'

'I reckon even a kid could make this.' Jack threw himself into learning what to do rather than over thinking. Over smelling. Over kissing. Overreacting to her every move. 'And this is difficult because?'

'Because you have an expert showing you. Oh, and I gave you the easy bit; I try to make desserts as fun and easy as possible for a lunchtime. As you saw, the chopping needs to be exact if the product is going to have the wow factor. And you haven't seen me assemble it all yet. Watch it—they all have to be perfectly symmetrical. I'm going to make a citrus wash to keep the fruit looking shiny, then we'll have to wrap them and pop them in the fridge overnight.' Having put a kettle of water on to boil, Cassie squeezed some lemon juice into a bowl then leaned against the counter. 'So where did you guys grow up?'

He hadn't seen that coming. She was only making conversation but still a swift stab of unease skewered his ribcage. 'Around.'

'I'll just leave this to cool.' She poured the water over the lemon juice, confident around the kitchen. Calm, even.

This was obviously where she felt the most comfortable. He'd never seen her so in control. Her gaze drifted over him, to his eyes, his mouth, softly. Gently. Memories of that kiss scooted through him.

God, part of him wished he hadn't said *never again.*

Her tongue dipped out to her bottom lip and her eyebrows darted upwards, giving him a hint to elaborate. 'Around where?'

Once again he gauged what to say. Always, he knew to give a little, enough to stop the questions. 'Nowhere for long. But I know all this area pretty much like the back of my hand—I did most of my growing up around here—Notting Hill, Latimer Road, Shepherds Bush, then a short stint in Camden and another in Harrow. Six, months I think. Then back here again.'

She laughed. 'Were you part of a travelling family, nomads, or your parents just got itchy feet a lot?'

'Something like that.' The juice on his hands was rapidly turning sticky. Washing them was a good distraction.

But clearly not for Cassie. 'Like what?'

'Like all of the above.'

She threw him a strange look. 'Well, and thank you for asking, I grew up in two houses in total. One in North London and then Chesterton. I moved here last year. I like it here, close to the market and the pubs and the Tube. Oh, and the Carnival. Do you go to the Carnival?'

'Not recently. I used to when I was younger.'

'I love it. It's such good fun. It's the highlight of my summer. All that great music, people so happy, dancing in the street, the smell of spice and smoke in the air, heavy bass beats echoing until late into the night.'

Her enthusiasm was infectious and he drew frail threads of memories from the back of his mind. 'One time I remember...'

Colours and scents, the happy, addictive atmosphere.
A new mother, a new family. A new start. All trying to do
the pretend family thing—a nice day out at the Carnival.

Then, the next year, different family, different mother.
Different start. Things not quite working out. Excuses.
Tears.

Tipping her head to one side, she watched him. 'What
do you remember?'

'A whole load of stuff you don't need to know about.'
Because it was enough just remembering that having an
attachment to anyone, relying on anyone, loving anyone
save his sister, had ended in hurt. He didn't need to voice
that. He just needed to heed it. 'Okay, chef, so these kebabs are piling up, waiting for your professional whizz.
What are you serving them with?'

'A choice of either chocolate or honey-yoghurt dipping
sauces, both of which are in the fridge already made. You
want to talk about that? Sure. A company in the West End
has signed me up to do a healthy eating day once a week.
My remit is to produce a casual buffet-style lunch for the
directors that is low in calories but tasty and satisfying.
The chocolate is the treat we all crave at the end of a meal
and the reward for the other stuff. High cocoa solids and
low sugar. And in tiny amounts. So don't judge me, okay?'

She didn't look okay; she looked hurt because he'd
changed subjects so rapidly. But he'd reached the end of
the whole *share it with the group* thing. Something they'd
tried to foist on him through Youth Services. He'd preferred sneaking into the back of the cinema across the road
from their futile meetings and losing himself in someone
else's life. His hadn't been worth examining in any kind
of depth. Except working out how the hell to extricate
himself from it.

But his younger years and his film experience had

taught him enough about how to read people and right now Cassie was simmering. Not in a good way. Crashing a pan into the sink, she turned to him, all businesslike. 'Have you spoken to Lizzie yet?'

Jack set to, threading more fruit as guilt hit him from all sides. 'I rang her yesterday. We're having a quick chat tomorrow afternoon in the Market Bar, Portobello. Four-thirty. Any chance you can come? On time? I have things to do afterwards. Meetings with clients of my own.'

'Meetings in the evening?'

'Yes. In the evening. My client's in the States and it was the only time that was convenient for us both to Skype. Could be a big job; I don't want to be late.'

Cassie's voice was still loaded with irritation. 'Of course I'll be on time, Jack. The last couple of times were aberrations to my normally strict adherence to the clock. I do know how to run a business. Does she know I'm coming?'

'Not exactly.'

'Does she know I'm catering? Oh, actually, am I catering? Did I get the job?'

There had been other, probably better, definitely more organised caterers. But none of them had had the verve Cassie brought with her, or the passion. He hadn't tried the kissing...though he doubted any would be nearly as good as her in that respect. 'If you can come to the meeting. On time. Yes.'

'Great. Thanks. Again, does Lizzie know?'

'Not exactly. Her cell battery died halfway through our conversation; it was all I could do to get her to arrange a time and place. That's Lizzie all over.' Matched by his inability to bring the subject up over the phone. Having Cassie there would act as a buffer too.

'Well, it would be good if you could phone her again and tell her I'm going to be there and why.' When she finally lifted her head to look at him, her eyes were shadowed. 'Just so we all know where we stand.'

If he knew that he'd be a happier man. Putting down the pieces of pineapple, he turned to her. 'Is something wrong?'

'No, Jack. I'm fine. I'm tired and I'm busy.'

And annoyed because of him. What would it cost just to share a little? It was easier to kiss her than to talk. Go figure. Kissing would mean he didn't have to face those searching eyes, the casual questions that he didn't want to answer.

But how easy to open up some of those memories that he kept locked away? He'd drawn a line aged sixteen. Freedom and autonomy. *Life starts here.* And he'd blocked off the past, apart from regular visits to Lizzie. Taken his future into his own hands, grasped control. Finally.

But he owed Cassie something. He knew about her father. A little about how that had affected her. And, even though she was reluctant to talk about paring knife man, he knew she'd had her fair share of tragedy.

'One time I was at the primary school just up in Latimer Road and we had a dance troupe in the carnival parade. Lizzie was in it, all dressed up in some kind of Caribbean outfit. I helped make the float. It was in the shape of a dragon and what the hell that has to do with Jamaica I don't know. We won a prize, though. I got one of those whistles that drives everyone mad. I think I almost blew it dry. Didn't know a whistle could actually stop working from overuse. Must have driven the estate crazy. Maybe that's why we had to leave.' He breathed out, wanting to add: *That was with the fifth family, I think—I started to lose count after a while.* But thought better of it.

So, he did a mental body check, apart from an over-excited heart-rate he was still okay. It was hardly an exposure of his soul, but it was something. And inside him a hard corner of his heart relaxed a little. It also dredged a smile from her, so it had got to be worth it. Even though he didn't usually do this. And would not be doing more. 'Maybe I'll go this year. If I've got time.'

'Make some time. You're the boss, aren't you?'

'Of most things. Yes. And if I'm extra careful they even allow me to use knives.'

She waved one at him. 'Not these, my boy—these cost more than my van. So make a date with your diary and get yourself there. It's a must-go thing. I love watching all those kids dancing. I have a food stall every year, on the corner of Ladbroke Grove and Lancaster Road. I get a great view and I love the buzz and the atmosphere. Plus I make a stack of money and a lot of friends.'

He grabbed at the chance to change the focus away from him. 'So you sell what kinds of things?'

Her eyes glistened with excitement as she ran her hand in the air as if reading a billboard. 'Gourmet Caribbean. *Taste of the sun. Fruit of the islands.* Chicken and rice. Corn. Mango mocktails. Roti. That kind of thing. Does a roaring trade. You should stop by my stall; I'll give you a good discount. Mate's rates.'

'I would have thought you'd give your workers something for free.'

'Nothing's ever free, matey. Believe me. You always end up paying somehow.' She flicked on her MP3 and calypso music filled the room. She started to hum as she painted the fruit sticks with the lemon juice and water. Then rustled in the fridge and pulled out a large blue and white china jug. 'This music is so uplifting, isn't it?'

Watching her backside jiggle up and down in those tight sweatpants was all the uplifting he needed. He looked at the kitchen clock. One-twenty. She was going to be exhausted tomorrow. Just like his libido. Up. Down. Up. Down. Very definitely up. 'Are we almost finished?'

'No. Not nearly—we have washing-up to do, for a start. And these all need covering, then there's pasta to cook and cool for the salad, tomatoes to roast... My list is still very long. But, first, I want you to taste a kebab with the chocolate sauce.' She offered him a fruit-laden stick, dripping in sauce. He took it from her hand—no way was he going to let her feed him—no matter how tempting. His groin could only put up with so much. But hell, he paused as she stuck a spoon into the jug and took a long swallow of the sauce. Her pupils widened and a soft moan came from her throat that was similar to one he'd put there only a couple of hours ago. 'Oh, my goodness. That is soooo good. Go on, try it.'

Sweet fruit juice squirted down his throat, coated in a rich, dark, orangey cocoa dressing. It was sugar with just enough bitter bite and promises and heaven.

As he ate she watched, her eyes never leaving his face. Her unfettered eagerness struck a chord deep in him, her mouth tipped up into a smile. His hands fisted against the bench top as he fought back an urge to run them through her hair, to smooth them over those curves, to make her moan again.

Any chance of a rewind to just before they'd made that hands-off decision? Because while his brain was full of good, safe and sensible ideas, his body was all up for bad ones.

She waited for him to swallow. 'Verdict?'

'Delicious. Yes. Delicious.' And the food? Yes. Great too.

'Excellent. I thought so. A sprinkling of crushed nuts and we're done.' She rocked to the fridge and bent to put the jug back in. When she stood she swayed a little, caught the edge of the counter to steady herself. Blood drained from her face as two fingers pinched the bridge of her nose. 'Woo.'

'Are you okay?' Dumb question. Heart thumping out of his chest, he was by her side in a millisecond, his arm round her waist, pulling her against him. A medical emergency called for body to body contact, not debatable. She was hot and soft, but fighting.

Her head rolled against his chest, her scent whacking him full-on in the solar plexus as she pressed against him to get her balance. For a second he wondered what it would be like to do this again. Comfortable. Close. No reservations or restrictions. To hold her so still, for her to hold him right back.

Rubbing her temples, she sighed, 'I just went a little dizzy, that's all. It happens sometimes when I'm tired. Low blood pressure or something. I'll feel better tomorrow after a good sleep.'

'Which will consist of how long?'

She glanced at the wall clock and whirled out of his grip. 'Four hours if I'm lucky.'

'So go and sit down and I'll make you a drink.' He'd make her even if he had to chase her round the tiny apartment.

'I haven't got time to do that.'

His hand was at her hair again, pushing back the strand that refused to do as it was told. Seemed it was a genetic thing that involved the whole body. 'Make some time. You're the boss.'

'Another joke? From you? This is becoming a habit.'

'I joke on a regular basis.' Actually, he couldn't remember the last time he'd had some pure unadulterated fun. Tense, deep, controlled, yes. Amusing films and watching the escapades of his documentary subjects—vicarious fun. But laugh out loud for himself? Not so much. He spent way too much time planning his next assignment, improving his skills, forgetting the past. Watching through a lens as others let go while he held on. His drive to succeed had taken precedence, with short sharp dalliances along the way with women as seriously driven as him. No time for frivolous. Just a quick one-two and on their way. Cassie was the first woman who'd made him laugh in a long time—and that was precisely because she didn't take herself so seriously. She made it look possible to chase a dream—and enjoy yourself doing it. Even after everything she'd been through.

'What, so you put it in your diary? Joke at three-thirty? Chuckle at three thirty-one? And who made you head chef?'

'I did. The current one is clearly incapable of making any rational decisions. She can take over when she's feeling better.' He took her by those stubborn shoulders and steered her into the lounge, dug out a space on the sofa and pushed her into it.

'No. I can't let you do this. Please don't. I don't need you to help me any more. I'll get it done.' But there was a rawness to her voice that tugged at his gut. Despite her previous willingness to let him help, she didn't want anyone working with her unless she could control it. He got that. He didn't do *anything* unless he could control it. Usually. Kissing pretty chefs excepted.

'Cassie, I'm not going to do anything that will sabotage your buffet lunch. Believe me, I know my limits. But I am going to make a cup of tea and tidy up. When you've got yourself steady again you can come back in and finish off.'

Her eyes glazed a little and he guessed she was getting dizzy again. 'Okay. Just for a minute.'

Having settled her in, he went through to the bombsite

of a kitchen and his stomach bumped into his boots. She was right—she had used just about every pan and utensil she owned and it would take the best part of an hour to clean up. So he flicked on the kettle and let calm settle over him. Then he found the comprehensive to-do list.

On top of a bank statement. That told him what he'd hankered to know but hadn't been his business. It was hers, and the huge debt too. No wonder things were getting hard to juggle. Why was she in such financial straits? It wasn't just silly budgeting. And it had something to do with her ex.

Not his problem. He had enough work to do running his own career.

Which was all well and good, but she was working herself too hard trying to do it on her own.

Still not his problem.

'Okay, bossy britches. Here's the tea.' He wandered back into the lounge with a tray to find her slumped across the sofa. Utterly beautiful and utterly asleep. A picture of stillness—surely the first time ever. Her hair was a puddle of red across a strikingly bright plaid couch. Her chest rose and fell slowly, one arm hanging limply on to the floor. Tiny noises escaped her throat as she exhaled. The room was a stark contrast to his own post-modern mews house, with its sharp corners and one colour throughout. With little furniture, it wasn't a home; it was a place he stayed when he was in town. But here, this was a home; it felt loved. She inhabited it in full glorious Technicolor. It was right for her—a crazy, chaotic cocoon.

Watching her in here, he felt a strange pull in his heart. Warm. A strong desire to help this wild woman. As if part of him could do that, as if part of him could fit. Comfortable.

And suddenly the urge to run swelled inside him. Because he knew that getting comfortable was always the most dangerous place to be.

'Not again. Not again. Not again.' Cassie looked at the soggy puddle of rubber that used to be a tyre pancaked against the pavement, and her heart dropped to her sensible work shoes. Stupid London roads. Stupid, stupid van. Stupid person, whoever had thoughtlessly left that broken bottle there. The one she'd missed when she'd scooted quickly into the corporate offices carrying heavy crates she could hardly see over. She glanced at her watch and her heart just about puddled alongside the tyre. 'Not again. Not again. Not again. Please, no.'

Stupid Jack Brennan and his stupid obsession with timekeeping. Sure, he'd been some kind of knight in chef's clothing—to mix a metaphor or two. He'd finished the food prep, washed up and cleared everything away and made a good shot at roasting tomatoes, then disappeared into the night. Now she owed him. A lot.

But turning up late again, especially to meet his sister and discuss the most important day of her life, was not the clued-up, business-savvy impression she wanted to give either of them.

Plus, she'd had a long talk with herself in the shower this morning and firmly decided that anything other than a formal relationship was crossing a line she wasn't prepared to cross.

Cassie had her game face on and it was staying there. Or at least it had until now, when all it wanted to do was crease into a crumpled fuzz and cry like a baby.

She climbed into the driver's seat and hit her head on the steering wheel. Twice. Then found her mobile and phoned the cavalry. 'Sash? Hey, how are things? Er…fine. Thanks. Except, I'm stuck on Long Acre with a flat tyre.'

Her sister's usually unruffled voice ruffled. 'Again? Cass, you really should get better tyres for that heap of junk you call a van. Seriously, let me buy you a new one.'

And be forever in someone else's debt? Not likely. Cassie was collecting debts like other people collected supermarket stamps. Unfortunately, there was no special bonus gift at the end. 'Yada-yada. Says the woman who drove a bright pink jalopy until she met Mr Rich and Famous. My van is great; it's just the gutter that's the problem.' And she had to admit to buying budget tyres because anything else was just out of her reach. She inhaled. 'Sasha, I'm in a weeny bit of trouble. Or will be. I'm supposed to be meeting a client over in Portobello in a few minutes. I'm going to try changing the tyre…or get a cab. Or try to beam myself over there. But I don't want to leave the car here. I'll get a ticket.'

'Okay—you've tried the AA?'

'I had to let the membership slide.' A man carrying what looked suspiciously like a parking ticket machine and important jobsworth headwear appeared in her driver's mirror four cars behind. She was only a couple of minutes over her expired parking time. He'd be okay with that. Yes, right, because London traffic warden compassion was legendary. Not. She felt as if she was being slowly squeezed underneath a giant ticking grandfather clock. 'If I don't move it there'll be a tow and a fine.'

'You want me to do a search and text you the numbers of some tow companies?'

'No, no.' That sounded expensive. 'I'm sure I can sort it, somehow. I have a spare tyre and some sort of toolkit thing in the back; I just don't know how to do it. But, actually…' She hauled in more air, hating that she was going to ask her sister to do this, but asking anyway. 'Would you be an absolute darling and call my client? Let him know I'm run-

ning a little late. He's got another meeting later and I don't
want to make him late for that. He'd never forgive me.'

'What? Me? Why?'

'Because I'm trying not to look like an amateur.' Another glance in the mirror showed her face covered in red
blotches, hair sticking out at all angles and dark shadows
under her eyes. Amateur? She looked like a bag lady in a
chef's dressing-up costume.

The ruffled voice turned into the bossy big sister's. 'And
getting me to do the dirty work tells him you're a professional, how? Who is it?'

'Jack Brennan.' It came out like a sigh. *Damn.* She
steadied her voice, lowered it an octave. 'Ahem. Jack Brennan.'

'Ahhh.' Her sister sighed too. 'Dreamy Jack with that
amazing voice? I could listen to him all day. Sure, I'll call
him; it'll be an absolute pleasure.'

'Down, woman. You are married. Second thoughts, I'll
call him myself. He's a total time freak and I promised I
wouldn't be late.' This was her last chance, she felt, with
him. It had to work or she could kiss goodbye to him and
his forty-nine dinner guests.

'I'm sure he won't mind. I watched him, you know. Last
night. His eyes never left you.'

His hands had done a fine job too. And his mouth.
Only it hadn't been enough. Never enough. And beyond
too much.

She glanced back in the mirror; now the red blotches
were developing red blotches and the traffic warden had
whirred his machine into action for the car three behind
her. 'Well, what do you expect? It's a very nice dress—
thanks for the loan.'

Sasha laughed. 'He wasn't looking at your dress—well,

not so much. He was looking at you. And very intently, I might say. I think there could be a *thing* potential.'

'No way. I couldn't. I just couldn't.'

'I don't know what's happened to you, but you are so not my little sister any more. It's not like you, Cass, to be so closed off with men. You're usually more than happy for a *thing*. *Thing* is what you do. You, my darling, are the *thing* queen.'

'I don't want a *thing*. Not with him or anyone else. I'm taking a break for a while.' For ever? That sounded kind of perfect. No complications, no one stealing her stuff, no one making wonderful gestures and treating her nicely in a gruff way and being a perfect gentleman. With a time fetish. Not to mention she was so over roasting-hot kisses up against her hallway wall.

'What exactly did happen with Patrick? You never said. One minute he was on the scene, the next gone. I know you tend to have a short attention span with men, but you went seriously quiet over him.'

'Oh, you know; the usual stuff. It wasn't me; it was him. Can we not talk about this now? I have a traffic warden breathing down my neck and a culinary emergency.'

She smiled reluctantly at the phrase Jack had used. The way he'd looked at her—Sasha was right—he'd hardly taken his eyes off her from the second she sat down. And the rest of the happenings of the evening had gone by in a relative blur for her too. Except she remembered very clearly how his eyes had been so dark and warm, and his smile had made her stomach dance, how he had looked so… Oh, please. She was a sensible twenty-six years of age, not a swooning teenager, and had already decided that this could not go any further.

If only she could get him out of her head, but he was hell-bent on staying there, grouching around, frowning at the messiness of her brain. Laughing at the whirls and kinks he caused in there.

'Cassie? So you're okay? I mean, not in any trouble?'

'No. No.' But her voice wobbled as she thought of the contract disappearing, of Jack and his kisses and her sorry mind that couldn't compute anything any more. She was in heaps of trouble. This was definitely not the time for a sibling confessional, but Cassie felt that if she didn't tell someone she'd explode. Perhaps her sister could talk sense into her. Then she remembered her sister had married the most unsuitable, unreliable commitment-phobe rock star ever. Sense was something Sasha had eschewed for the sake of love. But the words were already spilling from her lips. 'He kissed me. And I kissed him back.'

It was very unlike her sister to squeal. But when she did it was loud and messy. 'You did what? When?'

'Last-week-and-last-night.' If she said it quickly perhaps her sister wouldn't hear the sordid details.

'He kissed you twice? Why in hell didn't you tell me?'

'Because it took me by surprise. I was going to tell you as soon as I knew what was happening. Honestly. It all happened so fast. Then there was nothing. And then it happened again.' She didn't want to say the words out loud and admit that something was happening inside her too. That she'd found a man who intrigued her enough to want to impress him. And no, it wasn't just about the money. Because she was confused, dammit. 'There's a traffic warden breathing down my neck. I have a muddled head and a flat tyre and I'm running late.'

'You kissed him. And then you kissed him again. I want details.'

'No. No, I can't, not here.' Not ever. Seemed that the older she got, the less she wanted to share about her private life. Or was that because she was wiser now? And didn't even want a private life.

'You want to impress him. And that's why you don't want to talk to him and admit to being something less than perfect.'

It wasn't about being perfect. It was about trust—of her heart, of her decisions, and of him. And if she told her sister this she'd have to explain about Patrick and the stolen money and admit to keeping even more things from the one person who knew her better than anyone. She'd have to tell her about the agreement that neither she nor Jack wanted more. Now her heart snagged a little because the stark truth was that maybe, just maybe, she did. Against her better judgement. That was why she needed to avoid him and why kissing had to be totally off the menu.

That would necessitate a long sisterly conversation, which was not appropriate for the middle of a busy London street with a clock ticking and a mean-looking man with a machine whirring into action in front of her. 'No, I'm supposed to be cooking for his sister's wedding and meeting with her two minutes ago. I'm trying to make a go of this catering business and that's what I need to focus on. Not *things* with beautiful but grumpy men.'

'He's a dark horse, I'll give you that—I never quite felt like I had the full measure of him. Brilliant producer. Very efficient. But a little held back. During the filming he was—'

Cassie snapped. 'Please. I don't need to know anything more about him. I have to get to this meeting.'

'You know you don't have to work yourself to the bone, honey. We're more than happy to help you out; Nate could get you a little job—'

'Stop that right now. Stop trying to solve my problems.'

'What problems?'

'Nothing. It's nothing.' Okay, so she knew she'd just asked her sister to help her out with a tricky conversation, but there was a difference between occasionally asking for help and always having it foisted on her. 'Now, stop talking to me. I've got to either change into my Wonder Woman outfit or ask a very crabby-looking traffic warden how to change a tyre.' And, seeing as she'd left the Lycra knickers and tiara at home, she resigned herself to it being the latter.

After she'd spoken to Jack.

CHAPTER SEVEN

THE MARKET BAR, as always, was filled with a lively mix of stallholders and creatives. A large television screen relayed a local derby football game while people shouted above cheers and friendly jibes. A gem of a pub in the middle of the market with olde-worlde decor leftover from its nineteen-seventies heyday, it served good old-fashioned food and, apparently, decent tap beer. Which Cassie generally avoided.

'Wine, please. Chardonnay's fine—anything, really, so long as it's a big one. I think I need it. I'm so sorry.' She looked down at her oil-covered hands and wished she'd had time to give them a good wash rather than a scraping with an old handkerchief and a splash of sanitizer that had smeared things around rather than eradicate them at all. 'Thank you for coming to help me out. I really appreciate it. And for negotiating me out of that parking fine; he just wasn't listening to me. And I'm so glad you know how to change a tyre.'

Jack shrugged. His face was the mask it had been since he'd arrived in Long Acre, taken one look at the glass and shaken his head, disappointment smudged across his eyes. 'If I hadn't, then God knows how long you'd have been. And, just for the record, it does help to have a spare that doesn't have a hole in it too. If you're going to continue to drive that wreck of a van you should seriously think about joining a road rescue organisation. I know they cost a bit but you can write them off as a business expense. Also, try picking more suitable places to park.'

Her stomach curled into a tight knot. 'Like I said. Thank you. And sorry. But I was managing fine until you arrived—uninvited, I might add.'

'There was nothing *fine* about it.' The intensity in his eyes was unnerving. 'You had the jack at a very unsafe angle that could have killed you with one wrong move.'

'Maybe you should have left it like that then, with me underneath it. Taken a chance.'

His eyes narrowed, his voice even. 'Believe me, I was sorely tempted.'

'And I made you late for your meeting, for which I apologise. Again.'

'Meetings, plural. Yes, you did. I've cancelled the later one. This one is more pressing, seeing as we're running out of time.' He shook his head, and Cassie felt the deep sting of embarrassment. 'I sincerely hope you find some way of working to time, Cassie, because it's going to be a shambles of a wedding otherwise.' His eyes closed as if he was silently calling on some inner Zen to calm him.

Sasha was right, she realised with a shock—deep down, she did want to impress him. It was about trust but it was about being perfect too. And she was a long way off the mark. 'Thank you, too, for what you did last night. I couldn't believe it when I got up this morning and saw you'd put everything away and even started the tomatoes.'

'I found a recipe online and followed that.'

'It was so kind, and so above and beyond anything I'd ever expect. Especially from a kitchen slave.'

She couldn't help but allow a small grin at the relief she'd felt as she'd realised just how much he'd done for her, without being asked. And for which she'd repaid him by being late. Again.

His stance softened a little at that, the hint of a smile playing across those lips. Which left her feeling hot and bothered in too many ways. Because he was right and wrong. She had been late but it wasn't a crime or directly her fault and, whilst she certainly took all responsibility for what had happened—well, hell, no one had died.

The man needed to lighten up. When he did there were glimpses of a glorious sense of humour and he was a lot more sexy. Her earlier resolve was being sorely tested by the sight of him in faded jeans, a seventies rock band tour T-shirt and battered boots. Watching him tinker under her car, lying down on the cold hard pavement to change her tyre, arm muscles twitching and curving at the strain, had increased his sexual attractiveness three thousand per cent. She did not need him to look any more gorgeous than he had before. But somehow the relaxed clothes accentuated his features, gave them a darker, more edgy appeal. And gave her a sudden low down hot flush.

He was all kinds of frustrating. Hot and beautiful. Dark and stormy. Terse, yet emitting a kind of electrical current she was compelled to connect with.

His eyebrows rose. 'So how did the buffet go?'

Yes, work. Think about work. 'It went great, thanks. The fruit kebabs were a real hit. I even got a few *compliments to the chef* comments. So I thought I'd pass them along.'

Something flickered across his eyes—pride? Then it was gone almost as quickly. Strange to think that offhand praise would have any effect on a self-confident man like Jack. 'No worries. I'd ask for a pay rise, but I don't know what the going rate for kitchen slaves is these days.'

'Now, now, don't get above yourself.'

'He has a habit of doing that. Don't let him. Hey, big brother of mine.' The soft voice belonged to a petite willowy woman, all wide eyes and thin, delicate features. She wore a smock-style pink summer dress, long white-blonde hair loose around her shoulders and an open smile. She was the direct opposite of everything Jack was. Where he was tall, she was short. Where he was dark, she was almost Scandinavian in her colouring. His eyes were darkest brown, whereas hers were palest cornflower.

She was also open and relaxed. And full of smiles. Hard to imagine them coming from the same gene pool. But then Cassie wondered if she was biased, having two sisters with almost identical hair and eye colour.

The woman stuck out her hand. 'Hi, I'm Lizzie. And you are? Sorry, I wasn't expecting Jack to bring someone.'

So he hadn't primed his sister about the catering issue. Cassie shot Jack a look that she hoped told him they were even. 'I'm Cassie. A…friend of Jack's.' And now she was torn between telling Jack's dirty little secret or letting him squirm with righteous embarrassment. Squirming seemed much more enjoyable, given the circumstances.

He didn't look remotely flustered as he stood, kissed his sister on the cheek and wrapped her in a warm hug. 'Lizzie. Thanks for coming later than we'd planned. We got a little held up.'

We? This was a prime time to get his dig in. But he didn't.

Lizzie grinned again and massaged the back of his shoulders. 'No worries. Relax, my boy. Finally, we have you away from a camera. It's just good to have you here for a while. And Cassie, of course.' Now his sister shot him a look. This one was full of questions, which he refused to answer, with a minute shake of his head.

While he went to the bar for Lizzie's drink, Cassie tried

to make conversation. 'So, Jack tells me you're getting married. Exciting.'

'Yes. Not long to go now. I just cannot wait to have that man as mine for good. It's going to be such a great day. It's slowly coming together. Who knew there'd be so much to do for something we'd decided would be a low-key affair?' Lizzie gave a huge grin and it was easy to see how excited she was. There were few similarities between the two siblings; it was impossible to imagine Jack getting excited over anything. Intense, yes. Playfully, joyfully excited, no. 'It's nice to see Jack out with a girl. I don't often get to meet many of his friends; he's so busy all the time. Have you known him long? Do you mind me asking—are things between you...you know...serious? Just, the way you said *friend*, it didn't give a lot away.'

Cassie nearly choked on her Chardonnay. Barely a week, two kisses and an awful lot of distance. 'No. We are...er...it's a...' What? Business arrangement? That would only raise further questions.

'Cassie is a caterer. She's doing some work for me.' Jack arrived back in time and sat down. After he'd played with his beer mat for a moment, he turned to Lizzie. 'Actually, I asked you to come here because I wanted to talk to you about the food for the wedding.'

His sister sat up straight. 'Ah. The food. Yes.'

'Is that a good yes or a bad yes? Only—' he inhaled sharply '—I have hired Cassie to cater for the wedding.'

'Oh. Wow. That's...great. Very generous of you.' Although she looked far from thrilled. Lizzie's voice lowered to a whisper. 'Don't you think I can do it? Is that it?'

'No. That's not it at all. I'm sure you could do it really well.' He glanced briefly to Cassie for support. But she was giving none of it. This was his battle—she wanted him to win, sure, because that was where her money was coming from, but she shared Lizzie's frustration. She wasn't going to take sides. Jack turned back to his sister. 'I wanted you to not have to worry about it. It's just another thing on your list and I'm sure weddings are hard enough to organise as it is.'

'Jack, I'm not four or fourteen any more. You don't have to do everything for me or sort out my problems now. Or direct me, like you do your subjects. It would be nice if you could come out from behind the camera every now and then and see that I can manage.'

Hallelujah, sister.

'I know you can, of course. You can and do achieve anything you set out to. I just don't think you should have to manage when, er, cooking isn't your forte.' He stroked his sister's hand and his thumb ran over the inside of her wrist. It was a tender and intensely private gesture. Cassie noted a small silvered scar on his sister's inner wrist and knew exactly what it stood for. Clearly, there had been some trauma in Lizzie's life. Trauma that Jack felt deeply about. Perhaps that was why he was so overly protective.

Lizzie shrugged her hand away. 'Actually, I've had a few practice runs to make sure things work. How about you come round, Jack, and give me a hand instead of just throwing your money around? Let's see how well you work in a kitchen, considering the best you usually do is dish things up from a takeaway carton.'

Cassie stood, knowing just how well the man could work a kitchen. Or at least how well the man could look in a kitchen. Perfectly distracting. But it was time to leave the war zone. She'd done what she could; the United Nations could take over. 'I should go. Maybe you need to talk about this without me being around.'

Lizzie's hand was on Cassie's arm now. 'Sorry. Sorry. Do you have siblings? You'll know what it's like; we squabble but deep down we love each other. Please stay. If cooking is your forte then maybe we do need to talk. Jack can be blunt at times—he hasn't exactly learnt the art of diplomacy—but he does have a point. Has he chosen a menu? Does he even know what we like to eat? Callum's a vegan. Did you know that? His mum's diabetic. There's a whole lot more to it than picking eeny-meeny-miny-moe on a menu card.'

Jack rocked back in his chair and laughed. 'I told you she wouldn't take it well.'

'I'm just surprised, that's all. Taken aback, actually. And it's a very sweet gesture, I know, but you could have forewarned me. Especially so close to the actual day.'

Touché.

Lizzie leaned across the table towards Cassie, the sibling war over, for now. Hard hats could be removed. 'To be honest, he's right—everything I've ever cooked has been one big disaster, apart from beans on toast—which I can usually make without causing a fire.' She laughed, turning to Jack. 'You remember when we lived with the Mendozas? Or was it Mrs Forrester? Yes, Mrs Forrester in Kilburn. I baked a cake for her birthday and she said it was the worst thing she'd ever tasted. It was flat and stodgy and decorated so badly—I was too excited; I couldn't wait for the cake to cool, so the icing melted off onto the counter. Still, she never offered to help me bake another one. I guess we were shifted on too quickly to someone else. Or something.'

'Yes, well, Cassie doesn't need to hear about that.' Jack's mouth had formed a thin line, shutting down his emotions, his face.

Whoa. They were shifted on—to where? Living with other people? Why? What did it mean? Cassie's heart plummeted as she realised she was being privy to something intensely personal. Something Lizzie didn't appear too concerned about sharing, but something that Jack definitely didn't want to talk about.

It was hard not to jump to any conclusions, but there were pieces of the Jack jigsaw that were missing, pieces she wanted to fit together. Shouldn't, admittedly. But she couldn't help wanting to understand why he was like he was—on the one hand, severely protective and generous. On the other, dishearteningly annoying and grumpy—which she now realised was a self-protection thing. It was more about something deeply mistrustful or just plain hurt within himself than how he felt about others. He wore his wounds like a barrier. If only she knew what they were.

She scrabbled around to find some sort of less contentious middle ground while a million questions whizzed around her head. 'Hey, I know, Lizzie, why don't you tell me what you have already planned for the food? I can help you with some ideas, then, between us, we can work out a full menu. Anything you have already prepared we can definitely use and integrate into the meal; I absolutely wouldn't want anything to go to waste. I can give you some suggestions as to how to do some of the easy stuff. In fact—' she realised she was handing some of her potential profit right back but it felt like the better thing to do '—if you want, I could come and help you prepare some things. The trickier dishes, I can do on my own and bring them over on the day. We could sort of mix and match your stuff and mine and work out a budget to suit you both. How does that sound?'

Lizzie's eyes glittered. 'Oh. Wow. That sounds great. Jack, what do you think?'

'Seems we've reached a compromise.'

Lizzie clapped her hands. 'Now, that's a first for my big brother—are you sure you're feeling okay?'

'Perfectly.' He shrugged. 'I compromise.'

'Since when? Is it snowing in Hell? And Cassie—' she gave Cassie a knowing look, as if she was somehow involved in Jack's momentous bargaining '—are you sure?'

'Absolutely.' Sure she'd still make something from the event, but not as much as she'd planned. Why did she find this family so endearing, to the point of cutting out some profit just to help them? She was as bad as her father.

And now alarm bells rang out. Her father had been too distracted by the people, not the profit; meanwhile, his partner had bamboozled them all out of a lot of money. Patrick was from the same scumbag bloodline.

Ignoring the alarms, Cassie pulled out her trusty folder and began a long discussion with Lizzie, as Jack watched silently, his demeanour relaxing as the evening wore on. While Cassie's grew more fidgety and jittery, being close enough to look but not touch.

Menu decisions finally made, Lizzie finished her second drink then picked up her bag. 'Now, I have to go. Callum's meeting me outside; we're helping make a float for the Carnival and we have a session tonight round the corner in one of the warehouses. It's my design so I have to make sure I'm there. Are you going?'

Cassie nodded, Jack's sister was so vibrant and positive; she was a real breath of fresh air. 'Wouldn't miss it for the world. I have a stall there.'

'A food stall? Both days? Oh, fabulous. I'll be sure to come and buy something from you.' Lizzie stood to leave, gave her brother a swift kiss on the cheek. 'Wait, hang on—do you need any help?'

'I...er...'

'I could bring Callum, because you have to meet him before the wedding anyway; we can talk some more about the big day and generally have some fun hanging out. What do you think?'

Things had been so busy, she hadn't hung out in a long time. But it was so hard to accept help these days. Firstly, because she didn't want to be ripped off. And she was sure she wouldn't be; they all seemed like decent, honest people. But then, so had Patrick, with decent, honest credentials and a badge to match. Secondly, the least time spent with old brown eyes here, making her insides turn to goo and her brain turn to mush, the better. She'd allowed him to help yesterday and the end result was that she was even more in his debt. 'I don't know.'

Jack stood and, despite his casual attire, he looked every bit a man who knew what he wanted and was going to work damned hard to get it. Like last night, as he'd gripped her waist and taken her mouth. 'I'm sure Cassie has it all worked out just fine. She doesn't need us messing with her stall.'

Lizzie bit her lip. 'Oh, okay, sorry. I do have a habit of foisting myself on people. If you think we'll get in the way, that's fine.'

'No. I just don't...' *need to spend any more time with your brother.* She didn't know how long she could shore up those defences before she was begging him to take her mouth again, and any other part of her he felt like putting his lips on.

Lizzie shrugged. 'I thought it'd be payback for what you're doing for me. I won't touch the food if you don't want. I could just collect the orders and keep you supplied with cocktails. I can't cook but I make a mean margarita. But if you don't want—I understand.'

'No, let me think.' There was something about Jack's sister that was undeniable. And heck, taking orders and filling them at the same time was pretty tricky on her own. Plus she never got a break. It was a long day. 'Okay. That would be lovely. Yes. Thank you. Only I won't be able to pay you.'

'As if we'd expect that. You're doing us a favour; we can do you one in return.' Lizzie turned to Jack and rolled her eyes at his reluctant stance. Hands deep in pockets, eyes looking anywhere but at the women. 'Don't think you're getting away with it, Jack Brennan. You're coming too. If it wasn't for you, then poor Cassie wouldn't be in this situation.'

'What? It's a job; she's getting paid.' He opened and closed his mouth, clearly thinking better of arguing with his sister any more. Eventually he spoke. 'I'm probably working.'

'Well, don't. For goodness' sake, take some time out. You're getting grouchier by the minute. Be there to help Cassie. Or you won't be coming to my wedding.' She slapped another kiss on his cheek then disappeared into the crowd, her voice trailing in her wake. 'See you. See you on Sunday, Cassie.'

'I'm sorry about Lizzie—she doesn't mean it. About the wedding—I'm giving her away; she'll look a bit daft standing there on her own.' Jack walked Cassie to the door and opened it to the bright early evening sunshine. Those questions about his past were on the tip of her tongue, but he continued talking. 'She gets a bit carried away sometimes. She's a people pleaser, and with a penchant for the dramatic.'

'And clearly you're not.' It was said very tongue in cheek but he turned to look at her.

'No. I'm not. I stopped needing people to like me a long time ago.'

'Well, that's a good job, then.'

'Meaning?' He glanced at her out of the corner of his

eye and she caught the exact moment he realised it was a joke. And, not for the first time, she wished she could bring a smile to that mouth again and again. To smooth out those edges and find the real Jack underneath. Because she knew he was there. He just hadn't got the hang of totally letting loose. Yet.

'Meaning you are very different. I mean, really different. It's hard to believe you're siblings.'

'Well, she's twenty-six. I'm twenty-eight. She's a girl. I'm not. Cassie, do I really need to explain to you the difference between boys and girls?'

Outside, the long, hot summer day had turned a little cooler with a gentle breeze. The traders had packed up, leaving empty stalls along the road. Cafés and bars spilled out into the street, which was lined with an odd combination of summery hanging baskets, building-high billboard adverts and rough and ready posters for grunge bands. Old-fashioned barber shops rubbed shoulders with independent designers' quirky stores, as if the area hadn't quite got a grip on its real identity.

He walked her to the traffic lights on the corner, and she realised he was taking her home. Making sure she got back safely, when his house was at a tangent from here. It was still light and she was perfectly safe. And she knew she was annoying the hell out of him, but still, the need to protect seemed to just be an automatic reaction within him.

'Go on then, Jack. Tell me about the birds and the bees.' Showing her would be more interesting. The rush of heat at the memory of him letting loose in her stairwell threatened to overwhelm her. 'I'm so overdue that conversation. Maybe you could teach me a thing or two.'

'Oh, Cassie. You have no idea.'

'Try me.'

He smiled then—it was wide and free and full. And she realised she was a lot like Lizzie, a people pleaser. Had been since day dot, and had amassed a great deal of friends, drawn to the promise of fun like a moth to a flame. Friends she hadn't been too careful about, people who hadn't necessarily taken care with her.

Jack wasn't like that. He obviously chose people with the same amount of care he invested in his career and his work, if he chose any friends at all. But Nate respected him and so did her sister. Lizzie clearly adored him and he her.

So it was a slam in the chest to know she wanted him to like her. She wanted him to touch her again. To kiss her. To feel those arms around her, to have those eyes look at her with such intense passion and need. Because there was a real honest depth to him, and emotion too—hadn't she just seen him so tender with his sister? He was so different to anyone she'd ever known.

And, as if he knew exactly what she was thinking, he stopped, his hand on her arm, backed her against a wall. 'Don't look at me like that.'

'Like what?'

'The way you did last night. The way you did last week. Like you want me to kiss you.'

She held his gaze for a heartbeat. Two. Three. And fought the battle inside her to reach out to him and draw him closer. He was, once again, reluctant to give anything away, but his eyes were heated with the growing tension, the fire that had been simmering between them that just would not go out.

'Would that be such a bad thing? Right now? Kissing?' Oh, God, she was losing her grip on reality. She was on a street corner with the one man she should not be anywhere close to. The man who made her think things and do things against every damned rule she'd written. And almost begging him to kiss her.

'Yes. A very bad thing. Although I would enjoy every single second.' His thumb ran over her bottom lip, sending shivers through every single fibre in her body. 'It would be a disaster.'

'Why?' And now she felt like a prize idiot, putting herself out there to him. But one of them had to be brave here. She couldn't continue denying there was something happening between them. It was a living, breathing thing. A thing she'd tried to ignore, and which only seemed to be getting stronger, brighter.

He turned away and picked up his pace. 'Because you're a good person, Cassie. And there's a lovely light in your eyes that I don't want to destroy.'

She followed him. 'And why would you do that?'

'Because...I would. End of. And I don't want to start something I can't finish—that wouldn't be fair.'

'But if you know that, you can work on it. Surely?' And why the hell she was trying to convince him to do something she knew was all kinds of wrong she didn't know. 'You could try.'

'I've tried too many times.' Stopping at a junction, he looked towards the end of her street but his whole body language screamed that he needed to get away—and fast. 'Will you be okay from here? I should go.'

'No way, José. You are not walking away from me. Crikey, you've kissed me twice and I know, I just know you want to do it again. And more. So what's stopping you?' She gripped his wrist and led him into a small communal garden flanked on four sides by rows of pale terraced mansions; it was cool and had a scent of late summer. 'I know I'm a pain in the butt, I'm loud and I don't know when to shut up. I'm incessantly late and massively disorganised. But those aren't the reasons you're fighting this. Hell—' she looked down at his jeans, knowing that there were parts of him that could not pretend there was no attraction there '—I know when a guy wants me.'

'Come on, Cassie. Don't you have stuff you need to be doing? Filing? Ordering? Threading bits of fruit on a skewer?'

'I'm ordering you to be honest. Or…or I won't go to the wedding.' She hoped he'd take it in the way it was intended, a little fun to lighten things up. And not the petulant little girl whine it came out as.

Clearly not. Running a hand across that messy mop of hair, he sighed. 'That's entirely up to you, of course. But then you'd miss out on a fairly nice payment and leave us all in a hell of a mess. I've told you what I can and can't give you. I don't do this relationship stuff, and I never make promises I can't keep. Believe me, I've had enough false promises to last me a lifetime.' He dragged in a breath. Let it out. 'So I'm not going to play games with you, Cassie, but I'm not going to open every wound for you either. If that's what you want, then you're talking to the wrong guy. I've introduced you to my sister, I've done my bit and now I'm going home.'

And with that he turned and walked away, leaving her sitting on someone else's lawn, the damp grass seeping through her trousers and a twist of hurt seeping through her heart.

CHAPTER EIGHT

'JACK, COME ON.'

'Okay. Okay.' God only knew why he'd been convinced to do this. He'd spent the last few days holed up in the editing room, stuffy and hot and with thoughts never wholly on the job. Even working late into the night, focusing on the real things that mattered—his career, where he'd be next week, next month, next year—hadn't been enough distraction.

Truth was, work just wasn't enough these days.

Gritting his teeth, he followed his sister through streets thick with people wearing bright clothes and wide smiles. The air was heavy with a loud bass beat and the smoky spice smell of a distant Caribbean island. Every single person he brushed past seemed pleased to be here. Excited. Everyone swayed to a foreign rhythm that actually seemed to reverberate in his heart—a wild bouncing vibe that coaxed and cajoled and seemed to promise: *you're going to have some fun today whether you like it or not.*

And Jack didn't.

Not least because he had no idea how to face Cassie again. He wasn't a lay-it-on-the-line kind of man. He'd learnt to hold everything close. He'd had to. To be strong. To be independent. To survive on his own. And yet she made him want to give just a little bit of himself. And he was scared as hell as to what that might mean.

Plus, their last conversation had ended as a damp squib and he owed her. She'd given up some of her profit just to make his sister happy, when she hadn't needed to. The least he could do was stick to his side of the deal and turn up. Bring a smile too.

'Come on, Jack! Hurry up.' Lizzie danced along in Callum's arms—a waltz, a whirl, a huge grin. 'I want to show Cassie our float as it goes by. If we can get there in time.'

'She's probably not even set-up yet. Or in chaos. Or forgotten. She'll definitely be running late. You don't know her like I do.' Did he know her? Really? Deeply? Enough to be able to make more than a passing observation of her business skills—and the fact she was a damned fine kisser; not much more, really.

But his feet were moving quickly through the slow-paced crowd. There were people as far as he could see, stretching behind him up the road into the distance and in front, down to the Tube station and beyond, lining the pavements, cheering from balconies and roofs, clapping and singing as parades of children dressed in feathers and frills and hoops and bows gyrated and danced down the street. And everywhere that whistle sound that gave him half elation, half heartache.

There was a chance they wouldn't find her in the crush. But the moment his skin prickled and his head was turning to the right he saw her face—as if his body had some kind of Cassie-guided missile.

Surprisingly, her Sweet Treats stall was way more sophisticated than he'd imagined. Impressive, really: a huge awning in bold colours with a multi-burner grill stacked high with corn, sizzling meat on skewers—she clearly had a thing about those—and some bread wrap thing called roti, if the sign was anything to go by. His mouth watered, not helped by the moment he caught full view of her.

Her hair was in its usual scraped-back style, showing that creamy pale skin, freckles and big soft eyes to their best advantage. She wore a tight T-shirt with a vintage guitar emblem on it and the shortest of short knitted skirts in navy blue with a red trim. He caught a glimpse of her long shapely legs before she wrapped an apron round her waist—no sexy devil this time; it was just a simple professional navy and white stripe covering that gorgeous body.

And she was laughing. Her head tipped back, perfect white teeth revealed by her luscious mouth. Whoever the man was that was making her laugh, Jack wanted to immediately stamp on him. But then, he'd walked away from her more than once. Rejected what could have been a sensational experience. Rejected her. So he had no claims on who she spoke to or what she did.

As she caught his gaze her laughter stopped, she shrugged her hands into her apron pockets and did not look him directly in the eye. Considering it was a hot summer's day, it had suddenly got mighty cold. 'Jack. Hello.'

'Hey.' He needed to put that smile right back. 'This is looking great. How's business?'

And he was going to achieve a smile with that? Yeah, right.

'Selling a bomb, like always. I can't keep up with demand, so it's good you're all here. We have serious work to do.' She turned back to Lizzie and Callum, gave them both a hug and found them an apron each. She began a rundown of expectations and prices. Halfway through the talk, she thrust an apron into Jack's hand. 'See that box of corn there? I need you to shuck all the husks off into the bin, then rinse them through in that bucket if they need it. When you're done, we can put them on the grill.'

Looking at the huge box, his heart dropped. 'So this is what? My kitchen nightmare? Punishment by husk?'

'Punishment? I don't know what you mean. You offered to help and this is what I need doing. Callum and Lizzie are serving so I need a pair of hands back here.' But a smile played along those lips. Yeah. Punishment.

And, looking at that sweet butt, he had his own very clear idea about what his hands could be doing instead. Need slammed through him again as memories of how she'd tasted, how she'd felt in his arms bombarded his brain. He felt hostage, somehow, to her penetrative gaze that saw beyond everything he wanted to show her. To the knowledge she was troubled by something that was not her fault. That he could help her, and that she would never, ever allow him to. That she would bumble along in some sort of crazy mayhem, causing herself way more stress than she needed rather than accept anything more than a little help in exchange for a good deed.

'Look, there's my float!' Lizzie jumped up and down and pointed to a magnificent purple bird on the front of a lorry, its rich golden feathers stretched high into the air with tips like flames. In the open-backed truck a dozen or so small children wore headdresses, tops and trousers in a shimmering gold, and they beat steel drums in a steady pulse.

Cassie put her hand to her mouth as her eyes shone in admiration. 'Wow. That's amazing. Beautiful.'

Lizzie nodded. 'I'm so glad it worked out okay; I was a little concerned it might be a wreck. It's supposed to be a phoenix—I hope you can tell. Rising again, and all that. The school's just been saved from closure—it seemed fitting.' Lizzie ran into the group behind the float and began laughing and chatting and dancing.

Cassie watched and smiled, looking as if she was aching to join them. 'She's very talented. It's beautiful.'

Jack could barely find words. His sister had done that? 'First time I've seen her artwork in a long time. You're right; she is talented. Guess she isn't fourteen any more. She's a whole grown-up woman.'

'Is that a surprise?'

'It's a miracle. There was a time...' Boy, he didn't know why he was saying this to Cassie, as memories of finding his sister so limp and lifeless rolled back and clogged his chest. So he stopped. Tried to think of something else to say but couldn't. A small part of him wanted to tell her about his past, but there was no point dredging up a whole host of stuff he didn't want to remember.

It had taken him long enough to put it all behind him. But there Lizzie was, dancing and vibrant and alive. Getting married. All grown-up. Perhaps she had begun to heal. His chest tightened some more.

Cassie's hand was on his, warm and small but comforting. 'I saw the scars, Jack.'

Not the internal ones, and they were the hardest to deal with. Lizzie had dealt with it all in a different way to him. She'd released her rage and her grief and wore her scars like a badge of honour. She'd survived. He, on the other hand, had internalised everything, subsumed it to a tight, hard knot. He breathed out slowly. 'Yes, well, it was a long time ago. She's come a long way.'

And sometimes he felt as if he was stuck in the Dark Ages.

Cassie flipped a roti bread stuffed with spiced chicken and vegetables on the grill; it seemed that she didn't want to push him any further. For that, he was grateful. She looked back at the bird float as it disappeared down the street, strands of her high ponytail catching the sun and glinting fiery red. 'I like the idea of the phoenix; I guess we could all do with some second chances.'

Jack threw what felt like his three hundredth corn cob onto the fire. 'Does that mean I can get a promotion?' *Or more? A second chance?*

Which was a crazy notion. He was here for the day, then out again. But, given the wild thoughts he was having about her—scorching, out of control and, God help him, tender—in all honesty, he shouldn't be here at all.

She hit him on the backside with her tongs. 'Never in your wildest dreams, Brennan. You have to show me what you're made of before I even consider giving you anything more responsible to do.'

He laughed. 'You drive a heck of a hard bargain.'

'Yes.' Her shoulders clipped back and she gave him a faux evil stare before joining in the laughter. 'I like to think so.'

An hour later and he'd been promoted to grill chef. A hot and very demanding job way beyond his comfort level, which involved making sure things cooked through properly but didn't burn—it was a close-run thing. But he was near Cassie, and watching her work around a makeshift kitchen with such ease was more of a turn-on than the dancers' pumping and grinding out on the street. Although the sexy dance moves and the sultry music, coupled with proximity to her, was making him think anything was possible—even desirable.

The beer didn't help.

Three down and he found himself swaying to the catchy street rhythm. Him, Jack Brennan, who spent his life on the periphery of people, looked out at the smiling, dancing mass and envied them. Worse, he wanted to be like them. Just for a moment, to have that carefree spirit that seemed so out of reach. Today he didn't have the camera to hide behind, and that made him feel exposed, but strangely liberated.

Cassie came to stand next to him and did a little two-step dance move between waves to the crowd. 'Looks like you're enjoying yourself. Think I'll have to find you another job to remedy that. Now, what do I have that's really dirty? Messy? Stinky?'

'So, up to my armpits in corn husks or burning my butt off here isn't enough payback?'

'Payback? For what?' Her eyelashes fluttered. 'I don't know what you're talking about.'

'Last week?'

'Jack, you were being honest. And I appreciate that. I just wanted a little…more from you, by way of an explanation. But you don't owe me anything—I get that. I really do. Oh, there's Martha. Martha!' Thrusting tongs into his hand, she ran out to speak to a woman dressed in very high silver heels, a huge pink feather headdress and a very small glittery bikini. After a couple of minutes the woman had taken Cassie's hands in hers and was twisting her back and forth in a samba-type dance move. Cassie was woefully bad, but she didn't seem to care, losing herself in the music, her body swaying back and forth, and always, always with that smile. It wasn't that she couldn't dance. It was more that she didn't take herself seriously.

Whether that was to hide her embarrassment, he didn't know. But she did it with humour and the enthusiasm she seemed to inject into every part of her life. She was mesmerising to watch, her head tipped back, mouth open, laughing. Nothing like the sombre, sober dancing he'd done with women who wanted to press themselves against him, who moved stiffly from side to side—who saw a dance merely as a step towards bed.

The knitted skirt came to halfway down her thigh and the sight of those long legs made his heart stutter. As she moved, her T-shirt stretched across her breasts just enough to remind him of exactly what was underneath. The smooth skin, the responsive tight buds. The pull to her was like some kind of magnetic force.

'Go on. Before you drool all over the produce,' Lizzie whispered, taking the tongs and pushing him towards her.

'No—' Because he had the distinct feeling that if he touched Cassie it would be a spark to fuse wire.

Too late. With a jump, Cassie turned round and saw him, stopped short, eyes wide and disbelieving. 'You're dancing?'

'I'm moving, no big deal. Besides, I asked you to dance before, at the awards dinner, and you turned me down.'

'That's because I was going home to work, and I don't do stuffy men's dances. Which is what I thought was on offer. But this—you... In the street. With people?'

It was hardly bump and grind, and definitely not twerking, but he could feel the music as if it was running through his veins. And suddenly the only thing he wanted to do was to dance with her. Maybe he had spent too long standing on the sidelines as life went by, merely observing through a camera lens, watching people have fun, watching them dance, and not enough of his time actually participating. What harm could it do?

He held out his hands.

She blinked at his outstretched fingers. 'You want to dance, literally, *with* me?'

'The whole world is dancing together, Cassie. In fact, we look the odd ones by not doing so. So why not?'

'Because you confuse me. Not in a good way. Besides, I need to watch the stall.'

He confused her—heck, he confused himself. This was

not what he'd intended to do, but the music, the atmosphere—Cassie—were too addictive. He wanted to hold her. To have her in his arms, share that sense of fun and smile alongside her.

And no amount of pretending he didn't was going to cut it. Yeah, she was like an addiction. One that had kept him awake at night, just waiting for the next time he'd see her. One more. One more. And going cold turkey hadn't helped—if anything, it had made things worse.

If he'd thought he was out of his comfort zone before then, hell, this was the worst place he'd ever been. And the best. 'There's hardly any food left and Lizzie and Callum have it all under control. Look.' He waved over to his sister and soon-to-be brother-in-law, dishing up the last of the roti and kebabs. 'We just need to pack up. They can make a start.'

A shadow fell across her face. 'But the money...my things. I can't just leave.'

'Hush.' He took her hand and felt the electricity pass between them. His heart pounded in anticipation. Every part of him strained for her. 'They'll look after it.'

'No. What if they don't?'

'It'll be fine—trust me.'

'That's exactly what I do not intend to do.' Her eyes narrowed and she looked back over her shoulder at Lizzie and Callum, who seemed to be managing perfectly well.

Still, given her history, she had every right to be unsure. 'Just one dance, Cassie, and we can come back straight away. Let loose.'

She snorted. 'Really? From you? Since when did you become Mr Laid-back?'

'I'm trying hard to relax. If that isn't an oxymoron. Give a guy a chance.'

She pulled away. 'You've already had them. And blown them.'

'I'm fully aware of that. More fool me.'

For someone who usually calculated every move before he made it, he was fumbling around, surprised at how much it mattered that she understood he was out of his depth, that he had no clue what the hell was happening but that he was doing it anyway.

And for a man who prided himself on absolute control, that was all kinds of confusing. He was surprised too, at how much it mattered not to dance with her, but she was angry at him for rejecting her and she had every right to be, but he felt it, deep in his core.

It mattered. She mattered. This woman, who had been prepared to run this hectic, crazy stall on her own because she couldn't trust anyone else to help her. Who had kept whatever disappointment she'd felt as he'd walked away locked inside her. And yeah, so she'd given him the crappy jobs but she hadn't railed at him. She had just focused on the one thing that mattered more than anything to her— surviving the nightmare of impending financial ruin. She could trust his sister a little. Maybe she could trust him just a little bit more—he'd seen it once there in her eyes. A softening. But that had been days ago and she'd hardened herself against him again now, he was sure.

But, just like after the first kiss, and the second, he was struggling to maintain any kind of line here. 'Dance with a friend, then? A client that you need to impress? Someone who you have met a couple of times...*kissed*. And, Cassie, I am not going to pretend they didn't happen, but they don't have to define what happens next, or our reaction to them. Nothing does.' He took her hand again. 'Come on, just look at everyone having a good time. You deserve a bit of that. Right? Think how hard you've worked; you can't watch this all go by.'

'Sure I can.'

'Dammit, woman.' He wrapped his arms round her waist and undid the apron ties.

Her hand grabbed his fist. 'What the hell are you doing?'

'Undressing you. And nowhere near as much as I'd like to. Now shut up.' Throwing the apron to Lizzie, he prepared himself for a fight, slipped his hands under Cassie's knees and picked her up. Walked her to the centre of the road, ignoring her protests. 'You are going to dance.'

'My, my, you can be very bossy. I think I might have to demote you. Teach you a lesson or two.' Her gaze moved from his eyes down to his mouth and stayed there a second. The air around them stilled, the music going out of focus. His heart pounded against his ribcage. One more kiss. One more kiss would be the beginning of something. What, he didn't know. But there was that line again and he was teetering on the edge of crossing it.

Her eyes fluttered closed and he caught sight of sparkling silver-blue eyeshadow, thick lashes. Tiny worry lines. A face so beautiful, so etched on his brain that it made his heart contract. For a second he thought she was going to lean in and place her mouth against his.

Instead, she laughed, her eyes bright and glittering. 'Okay, let's dance. Seems I have very little say in the matter.'

It was just a dance. In the sunshine. With a zillion other people around. So it didn't mean a thing.

Neither did the long, slow caress of her body against his as he gently put her down on the ground. The hardness of his body as her bottom slid over him.

Or the tingle through her nerve endings as he spooned behind her, heat against heat, skin on skin to grind down the road. There was something irresistible about a take-control man. Especially knowing how hard he was fighting this attraction and failing. She'd made him pay his penance for walking away and it made her feel excited to know that he had done that to protect them both from something he felt was out of his control. She just didn't know how to handle it. Because ignoring it wasn't working; it was too big for them both—an attraction, a connection that they couldn't pretend wasn't there. A phoenix rising, strong and doubly potent. Even when her head told her to stay away from him, her body craved him.

He pulled her close as they edged down the road, following a slow-moving truck with blaring music. All around them people writhed against each other in time with the beat that had attached to her heart and was pumping loud and fast.

'Just as far as the Tube station, then I'll go back to the stall.' Main thing was to keep an eye on her money, not on his backside dressed in faded jeans. Or that T-shirt-clad chest that her hands itched to touch.

'Whatever you want, Cassie.'

She didn't know what she wanted—apart from him. On her lips, in her bed. Inside her. Just thinking about that made her abdomen contract in waves of want. And still the boom-boom steady rhythm vibrated around them, her breathing ragged with exertion, her arms swinging in the air in time to the music, his hands stroking down her inner arm, her outer thigh, her hip. 'This is so not old man's dancing.'

His mouth was so near her ear. Kissing distance. 'If any old man started doing this to you I'd punch him out.'

'My hero.' She pretended to swoon.

'If the badge fits.' His head tipped back and he laughed, a real deep laugh that came from his belly. It was amazing, really, to see him so free from the constraints he put on himself. The control. The edges he made for himself. When this…this was nothing short of beautiful.

The truck came to an abrupt halt and so did they, clashing against each other. Jack slammed up to her. 'Whoa. Got carried away there—sorry.'

'Don't be.' And all she was aware of was this conflicted man who gazed at her with possession in his eyes. Her arms curled round his neck and he didn't protest and neither did that tiny voice of doom in the back of her head. Because they both knew it was the atmosphere and the music that was making her feel fresh and fun. Oh, and possibly Lizzie's wicked margaritas. And being so close to him.

She knew his boundaries, that he didn't want more, couldn't commit. And hadn't she already promised herself that there would be no more from her? But fun wasn't off the menu, not after a hard day's work. In days gone by she'd have played happily without any thought for tomorrow. Maybe she could do it again.

Today was Carnival. Party time. She looked around at all the people in their fancy dress, laughing and smiling, shrugging off the drudgery of everyday life. Everyone wanted just a little bit of fantasy for a day or two. Come Tuesday morning, there would be responsibility enough. It had been too long since she'd had any fantasy for herself. 'Any time you want to body slam, I'm your girl.'

'Cassie, there are plenty of things I'd like to do with your body.' His arms slid around her waist as he pressed close to her.

Her heart tripped. 'You want to tell me?'

'I want to undress you. Slowly. Very slowly. And take my time getting to know every inch.' His mouth was near her ear and she shivered against the hot breath on her neck. 'But first I want to taste you again.'

Twisting her head round ever so slightly, she felt his lips on her skin. Twisting further, she found his mouth with hers. Then she was fisting his T-shirt in her fingers and pulling him to her. Blood pounded in her ears as a pulse throbbed in her groin. Low and hot and urgent.

His fingers meshed in her hair as he took her mouth in another breathless open-mouthed kiss that she didn't want to end. The way he made her feel defied all logic, her earlier resistance just a fading memory.

As he opened his eyes the music came back into focus and she realised the truck had moved further down the street. But she didn't want to move, not a single step, without this man holding her. She looked up into his face, a mixture of relaxed and sexual heat—a degree of frustration of the sexual nature.

His deep voice tripped mini explosions in her stomach. 'Do you want to get out of here, Cass? Your place is closer.'

She knew exactly what he was asking, and that he couldn't offer her more than a night, possibly the rest of the weekend. That afterwards he would walk away, uninvolved and probably unscathed.

Could she?

God, for so much of her life she'd been the one who called the shots. Bossy little sister who got what she wanted. Spoilt teenager who twisted boys round her finger. Then she'd been burnt and all her buried insecurities had boiled over. This would be a chance to take control of this part of her life. To find that fun girl again, to play a little. Because all work and no play was making her feel very dull indeed.

His fingers smoothed down the back of her neck, over

her shoulder, sending shock waves of want through her. 'What do you say, Cassie?'

'Yes. Yes.' Her eyes never leaving his, she offered him a consenting smile and with that the tacit promise that this would be the uncomplicated deal they both wanted. 'But what changed your mind?'

'Look at you.' He tipped her chin up and placed a kiss on her cheek. 'You have to ask?'

Then his mouth was on hers again, taking her as if he had a thirst he couldn't quench. And she gripped him, even now wondering what foolish idea this was. But dismissing it anyway, because there was no way she could resist that taste, that heat and that promise of more.

But first she had to deal with the rest of her food and clear away her stuff.

Turning to look back up Ladbroke Grove, she saw her stall, the banner bright and happily flickering in the breeze. But no customers, no servers. The parade had long since passed and stragglers wove their way down the road, discarded cups and paper littered the pavement. No sign of Lizzie and Callum. Or her money.

Now there was a more violent pounding in her ears. 'Where are they? Where's my cash? Jack? Can you see them?'

'No. No, I can't see them.' He squinted into the sunshine. 'But don't worry, they won't be far away.'

South America was the place of choice, apparently. The thump-thump-thump of her heart sinking in her stomach made her nauseous. Reason told her that he was right, but experience reminded her that not everyone had the same trusting heart that she did. 'Why did I let you talk me into a dance? I knew...just knew—'

'Hey, Cassie, please. That's my sister you're talking about. I'm sure they'll be here. Wait—over there?' He pointed across the road towards her van. Still no one familiar. 'Maybe they're packing up. Or something.'

'Or something? Do you think they left the cash box there, out in the open?' Running over to the stall, she searched underneath the counter. Between the empty boxes, on the floor. Her hard-earned money. Gone. Again. All because of another man. Images of those damned red numbers floated across her vision. She'd let her guard down too much. 'Do you think someone's taken it?'

'Calm down, Cassie, stop overreacting. They'll be here somewhere.' He scanned the road and pointed at two figures sauntering towards them from the corner shop across the road. 'See? Look, there they are.'

'Thank God. Thank God.' Air whooshed out of her lungs as she let relief spread through her. Because she couldn't face losing any more. Not her money. Not the trust she was just starting to build. Not her heart.

She looked over at Jack, with his arm around his sister, waving the money box at her. His smile was rueful and not as bright as before. Her overreaction had hurt him, she was sure, and she immediately felt bad about jumping to conclusions about his sister. But, quite simply, she had to put herself and her business first.

As he neared, she remembered the feel of his fingers on her skin. The thrill of what they'd agreed. The joy of seeing that face spread into a smile. Something inside her swelled just a little more.

Seemed as if her heart was already a lost cause.

CHAPTER NINE

'TELL ME, CASSIE, what the hell just happened. Because there's more here than you're letting on.' Jack was trying to be reasonable but knew his voice was just a little fraught, a little too loud. Okay, so Cassie was under pressure—he'd seen the bank statements for himself—but that didn't mean she had carte blanche to accuse his family of some ridiculous crime.

That she hadn't trusted Lizzie annoyed him. And put the promise of more hot kisses so far on the back burner the light had gone out.

Stacking the now cleaned boxes and cooking utensils into her tiny spare room, she put her palms up, her chest heaving with exertion and frustration. Her jaw tensed as her gaze hooked on his and didn't budge. 'Leave it, Jack. I overreacted and I'm sorry. I should know better than to behave like that. Your sister is lovely and she genuinely wanted to help. I feel bad that I doubted her.'

'So explain it to me. I'm all ears.'

'Oh, and this from the man who never quite manages to finish his sentences before clamming up or changing the subject. That kind of explaining?'

Typical—trying to change the focus away from her. *Right back at you, kid.* 'This is important, Cassie. I get that you don't trust me, but I hoped we knew each other better than that. She's my sister. I'm your client—'

'Thank you for reminding me exactly where that line is drawn. And thank you for helping me; we seem to be done here, so you can go.' She walked him to the front door. But he would not leave while this hovered between them. He could find another caterer, but he doubted he'd find one as passionate as Cassie. Plus, spending time with her today had just about convinced him that she was organised enough to manage a wedding.

Had. Did he really want someone so untrusting to look after his sister's needs? He didn't know.

And this was nothing to do with the dancing, or the laughing or the kissing. Or the A to Z of emotions ricocheting across his chest.

Okay, so it was everything to do with that.

He could pretend he didn't care but the truth was—and this was the real bummer of the situation—he did. Which was the very reason why he should take heed of her and go. 'Absolutely no way. I am nowhere near finished. Not everyone is out to get you, you know. If you carry on with that attitude you're not going to get far in your business. Or your personal life.'

'Thanks for the heads-up. Must try harder—okey-dokey. I'll add it to my very long to-do list.' She looked as if she'd been stung. She looked exhausted, hurt, drawn. Her hand went to her cheek, her face reddening.

It wasn't his intention to hurt her. But her steadfast reluctance to talk was irritating. He controlled his voice. 'That's not what I meant. You're doing everything right for your business. Honestly, no one works harder than you. But why the need to do it all on your own? Why the lack of trust that anyone can do it with you or for you? Why not let people help if they can? Nate could hire you an assistant or even bail you out the cash you owe; it'd be a tiddly amount for him.'

'You really don't get it, do you?' She let out a deep loud sigh and stomped through to the lounge, where she sat down heavily on the sofa, head in her hands. 'Because I want this to work on my terms, not because my big sister organised it for me. Or because some man swoops in and tries to take over—believe me, I learnt a hard lesson there. Have you any idea how much it rankles to be babied? For no one to take you seriously?'

He knew how it felt when no one listened, if that counted for anything. 'Tell me.'

She stared at the wall as a battle raged behind her eyes. 'When my dad died they tried so hard to protect me, some kind of misdirected focus of grief, I think. They even stopped me from going to his funeral in case I got too upset. Can you imagine? Dumped me with the neighbour while they actually did something with their grief. I just had to swallow mine. I was his baby—something I always cherished. *Baby girl*, he used to call me when I cuddled up on his knee. He was everything to me. I adored him—he was big and brave and my total hero. I couldn't work out what had happened when he died—only that he'd gone, and I missed him so much. But I wasn't allowed any grief of my own.' Her eyes glittered with tears but she blinked them away. 'I never got to say goodbye.'

'Oh, Cassie, I'm so sorry.' To have someone you looked up to, who cared for you, ripped away and never have the chance to ask why or to say how you felt about it—like having a mouth gag, your voice muffled and unheard, no matter how much you tried to scream or shout. Yeah, he knew how that felt.

'You don't have to be sorry; it was a long time ago and they meant well, really. I understand that, but it got out of control. *Don't let Cassie hear about any problems. Don't let Cassie face any sadness. Let's all pretend we're living happy families.* And any discord was always out of my ear-shot. As a teenager, I came to relish all the positive attention, and then, over the years, grew frustrated by it. But, ever since, I've taken little responsibility, always knowing that if I failed I'd have someone to bail me out. I was a spoilt kid who didn't take anything seriously until I finally worked out what I wanted to do with my life. Hence Sweet Treats. I want to prove to them that I'm capable of doing something substantial. Most of all, I want to prove it to myself. That I am substantial.'

'Did it ever occur to you that they do this because they love you? Because they want to protect you?' All he'd ever wanted was a family who'd stick by him. So he'd made his own with his sister. And he'd been as guilty as Cassie's sisters, trying to ease the way for Lizzie in a genuine belief that he was doing the right thing. But even then he almost hadn't managed to save her.

'I know they do. Of course.' She managed a soft smile. 'We're very close. It would hurt them deeply if they thought I was frustrated by them. So I need to show them, not tell them, that I'm a grown-up now. If Sasha had her way I'd be working every day for her charity, where she could keep an eye on me.'

'Do they know about what happened with Patrick?'

'No. And I don't want them to know. I don't want them to think they can charge in and rule my life again. Or give him the satisfaction of ever finding out how much he hurt me.'

'What exactly did he do to you?'

She shook her head, her breathing becoming rapid as her forehead settled into a heavy frown. 'He knew best, he said. How many times have I heard that in my life? Everyone always thinks they know best. He certainly knew a lot and made me think everything he did was for my own good. I believed him. I trusted him, because I had no reason not to. I'd never met anyone I couldn't trust before. He helped me set Sweet Treats up and ran it for a year or so, which gave him ample time to steal all my money, plus some more from the bank. He organised an overdraft in my name—and with my signature, which I absolutely regret giving—and withdrew to the limit. Then disappeared. Gone.'

'Bastard.' Jack's hands fisted involuntarily at the way she said it so matter-of-factly, but he didn't miss the darkened eyes. She was trying to make light of it, to show she was moving on. Surviving it, more like, because he knew how much she was in arrears at the bank. 'Can the police do nothing about it? What about the bank? Surely they want to recoup the costs?'

'They're trying to track him down but he's left the country. Oh, and to add insult to injury, he'd been a policeman, once upon a time, so he knew exactly how to cover his tracks. Now I'm working out a way of paying the money back, plus trying to run the business to a profit. What makes me so angry is how little I allowed myself to see the real him, wanting to believe some kind of romantic fairy tale. I'm gutted that I was so trusting with my livelihood. I won't be making that mistake again.'

But this was a woman whose father had been misled and betrayed too. Whose flaws had been splashed across the national newspapers and who had been accused of either blinkering himself or, worse, collaborating in a dreadful fraud that had affected so many people. If anything, Cassie was probably afraid to be compared to her father. She raised her palm up and shrugged. 'What is it that makes people think they can treat me like that? Because, really,

I have no idea. I am so sick of having no control. Am I so damned insubstantial?'

'No way. You are one hell of a woman. Strong, ballsy and very, very beautiful.' His gaze caught on to hers again and something unspoken tripped between them. The atmosphere in the room crackled with tension—an urgent sexual need mixed with the host of emotions hammering against his ribcage. Admiration at the woman who was trying so hard to be what she wanted to be. Anger that she'd been cheated out of her hard-earned money.

And lust, pure and raw, fizzing through his veins. He tried to focus on her eyes instead of the breasts that rose and fell with her impassioned talk. Or the legs peeking out from the short skirt he wanted to rip from her.

He stepped towards her, not knowing where this would take them, but not caring. He couldn't think of living another moment without having her. Without feeling her sigh beneath him. He touched her cheek, her lips, fingertips smoothing over the soft skin. Then, without thinking at all, he pulled her from the sofa, crushed her to him, his lips meeting hers with a force that snatched his breath away. He could no more walk away from her than douse the feverish heat that had built inside him since the first second he'd laid eyes on her.

She tasted of margaritas and sunshine, of fire and ice, of passion and heat. His hands skimmed her body that softened against him, the promises they'd made earlier reaffirming themselves in the press of her breasts against his chest and the tight moan in her throat. Her hands roved over his back, gripping his shoulders as the kiss deepened, taking them from warmth to bright heat, from promises to a pledge.

Finally, she pulled away, breathless, her lips swollen from the kiss, her hand travelling down his shirt. 'So, hey, Mr, I'm rebuilding and taking control of my life. Be very careful because from now on I get to call the shots.'

And that sounded very interesting indeed. 'Hey, control is my MO. Should I be scared? Or excited?'

'Both.' She grinned, took hold of his hand and led him into her bedroom.

As she closed the door and leaned back against it, Cassie tried to steady her erratic breathing and the sharp burst of sexual anticipation that seemed to render her incapable of moving any further. She looked up into those dark brown eyes, almost liquid with heat and desire, and her body responded, not with the confidence of the words she'd just said, but with a fierce trembling that made her feel weak and strong at the same time. Her heart thumped and danced.

Jack wasn't a man who would easily relinquish control. He grabbed one of her hands and held it above her head against the door, dominating the space, his muscles bunched and rippling. His other arm lifted and she was trapped beneath him, penned in between the cold wooden door and his body. His smell bewitching her—all she could see, all she could hear, all she could breathe... 'Jack—'

She wanted to tell him that she knew this was for only one night. That she understood. That she would be fine. That she didn't want anything from him except pure physical satisfaction because that was all either of them could give.

But she couldn't find any more words. Just one.

'Jack.' It was enough. It was too much. 'Jack—'

'Shh.' He smothered her words with his mouth, nipping and biting her bottom lip until she was incapable of thinking of anything except him. His heartbeat against hers. His lips against hers. His skin against hers. His body pressed against her and she rocked against his thigh, desperate to feed the ache in her core. She was ready for him. Wanted him. Her breasts grazed against his shirt, nipples pebbling with an exquisite sensitivity.

One hand dropped to her skirt and his fingers found their way across her inner thigh to her hot damp centre and she gasped with pure delight as he pulled aside her panties and stroked her nub. She lifted one leg around his thigh, her body flushed with more heat and more and then his fingers were sliding inside her and her brain short-circuited. His mouth now exploring her neck, kissing and sucking until pure sensation after sensation rolled through her and she called his name again and again with increasing urgency.

He stroked her hair as she gave in, as she shattered into pieces, bucking against his hand, not wanting him to stop, wanting him inside her. Wanting him. 'God, you are amazing.'

Struggling for breath, she laid her head against his chest, pressing kisses amongst the light smattering of golden hair. 'Whoa. That was…unexpected.'

'See what happens when I call the shots?' His heart was still racing against her ear.

'And you will pay for your insubordination.' She lifted her head and gently bit down on his bottom lip, saw the flare of unbridled lust in his eyes.

He swiped the back of his hand across his mouth, looking for blood. He didn't find any. 'Yeah? We'll see about that.'

When his arms caught under her legs and he picked her up and carried her to the bed she let him lay her down. He climbed alongside her and when he kissed her again and again with a tenderness that almost made her bones melt she forgot about who was supposed to be in charge. It was an equal need. An equal fever. Giving and taking. As the kisses intensified she matched his heat with her own, her tongue meeting his in an age-old dance that stoked the long slow burn in her belly.

His fingers trailed over her T-shirt, tracing tiny circles over erect nipples that strained for his touch. For his tongue.

When he finally reached behind her and unclasped her bra she could barely breathe with the anticipation. With a smile, he pushed off her T-shirt, let the bra fall to the floor and then his mouth was on her breast, his tongue lapping tiny strokes that lit fireworks in her gut and made her moan with exquisite pleasure.

She tugged at his shirt, tried to pull it over his head, wanting him naked, wanting to see the body she'd felt under her fingertips.

'Wait.' His hand covered hers, his voice back in take-charge mode. 'Cassandra, we've got all night. Slowly. Slowly.'

'But I command you, kitchen slave. Take off your clothes.' She didn't want slow. She couldn't get enough of him, of that hard body pressing against hers, of his erection pressing into her abdomen. She wanted it pressing inside *her*. Waiting was torture. Intense pleasure and matching torture. Doubled by the trail of his tongue down her belly to the waistband of her skirt.

'One thing at a time. Now, this is extraneous to requirements.' He pulled her skirt down over her thighs and paused for a moment as she lay there, exposed and breathless. His eyes locked on to hers and she saw in those dark pupils a desire that matched hers. That glittered with need.

His gaze scanned her body, travelling from her face to her breasts, then lower and lower, his eyes heating with every inch. 'You are so beautiful.'

'Stop looking and do something before I explode.'

'Looks like I've got me one bossy woman. I say hell, yes to that.' He laughed and dipped his mouth to her hip-bone, placing hot wet kisses down to her thigh, and dispensed with her panties. Her fingers tangled in his hair as he parted her legs, his breath whispering over her opening. Then his tongue tasted her, licking her, making her tremble and writhe against his mouth, at the very edge of perfection.

'Don't stop. Please don't stop. Please—' When she thought she could barely hold on any longer, he stopped. She fisted his hair. 'What did you stop for?'

'Oh, you know. I like to hear you beg. Say it again: *please, Jack.*'

'Not on your life. Never. Not if I was desperate.' He licked her thigh and she moaned.

'Cassandra, you are desperate. For this.' He licked again and hot blissful waves rippled through her.

'Never.' She couldn't help the laugh; she tugged a little on his hair. 'Two bosses are so not going to work. Come on, give in. Take your shirt off.'

He paused for a second then finally shrugged off his shirt and she saw the magnificent defined muscles underneath. Her hands went instinctively to his chest, smoothing across the skin, pulling him close, flicking her tongue against his nipples, watching him squirm with pleasure. Skin against skin, heat against heat. She rubbed against him, every inch of her body wanting contact. His mouth against her neck, his hands grasping her bottom, his hardness a tantalising desperate tease against her pulsing opening. She wanted him. Now. To fill her, to rock against her. Inside her. Deep inside her.

She couldn't wait.

Now.

He reached for his jeans zip but she stopped him with her hand. 'No.'

'Yes.'

'Tut-tut. Do I detect more dissent here? This is mine.'

Before he could answer, she was on her knees, tugging down the zip and throwing his jeans to another corner of the room. She took his erection in her hand, big and hard. And all hers. She ran her fingers down the length of him, then stroked over his tip as he tipped back his head and groaned.

Then his tongue was filling her mouth and he was pushing her back on the bed. Within a second he was sheathed and inside her, stretching her, filling her. He cupped her cheek with one hand as he shifted her bottom to a better angle with the other. Deeper he plunged, harder. Faster. She felt the pressure begin to mount again, her climax just out of reach as ripples of heat shivered through her. Nearer. Faster...

Jack groaned as he felt the sweet heat of her clamp around him. He pushed further, seeking a rhythm that held his own climax at bay until she reached hers. Her eyes fluttered closed as her mouth fell open. Tiny whimpers of pleasure escaped her throat. She lifted her head, pressing against him, her fingers scraping down his back. The hot sharp pain as her nails pierced his skin fuelled his need. He was losing his grip. Losing himself in her. Losing control. And he didn't care. All he wanted was this woman. *This.*

Finding her mouth again, he kissed her hard, rocking against her. But she twisted underneath him, slid away from him, releasing him, hard and hungry, against the cool night air. With her fists against his chest, she pushed him back on the bed, her eyes alight with lust. 'My turn on top.'

'Now this kind of bossy I could live with.' He reached for her but she dodged out of reach.

'Oh? How much do you want it?' Her fingers trailed across his erection, stroking and squeezing in long slow movements. One more. One more. Any more and it'd be too late.

'Oh, God. No. Cassie, don't—'

Her mouth was near his ear, her breath hot, her nipples brushing against his arm. 'Now I want to hear *you* beg.'

'For heaven's sake, woman.' He pulled her delicious naked body down on to him. 'I will not be responsible for what I do to you. But you have been warned.'

'Promises, promises, Mr Brennan.' Then she straddled his hips, positioning herself over him, her tight velvet walls closing around him, releasing him. Closing, then releasing. Up and down. Up and down. Starbursts of pleasure exploded in his gut, in his head, in his eyes, every pore sensitive to her smell, her taste, her touch. He cupped her breasts in his hands as she bucked on top of him. The rhythm sped up as her face creased into an ecstatic smile, she sank and rose over him until he was gripping on the edge. One more...one more...one more.

'See, Jack, look what happens when I'm in control.'

He had to hold on. Had to hang on to that single thread of control. Until he felt her tighten around him, his name on her lips again and again. She fell against his chest, her breathing rapid and erratic, covering his mouth in a wet, fevered kiss that spun him sideways, upwards and spiralling out and out. Then, shaken irrevocably, he roared into the darkness, his control blown to smithereens.

CHAPTER TEN

'OH, NO, NOT again. Not again. What time is it?' Cassie blinked, suddenly wide awake as fingers of bright sunshine streamed through the blinds into her bedroom. She jerked up and peered at the digital display on her mobile.

Damn. Late o'clock. Story of her sorry life.

But—oh. Her heart stuttered and jumped, her bones aching after the unusual nocturnal activity. She had a heck of a reason this time. 'I'm late again.'

'No surprises there; tell me something else that's new.' Beside her, Jack turned over and slipped an arm round her waist. The sheet barely covered his nakedness and she allowed herself a couple of seconds to just look at him. He had all but worshipped her last night, taken his time to make love to her exactly how she wanted him to. Hot, wild and glorious memories tripped through her brain—a perfect night of fun, laughter and intimacy. Then, the last time, he'd lain opposite her, stroking her so softly, staring into her eyes, and the orgasm had taken her to a place she hadn't known existed.

She'd discovered a lightness she hadn't known Jack had. A lightness she liked. More's the pity, because she did not need to find anything else to like about the man. He was the order to her crazy. The sense to her silliness. And a genuine tenderness too. Something rare in men she'd dated before. But the stark truth was—he was also out of reach and not something she had the time to be grasping for right now. A delicious distraction from what was important.

He nuzzled against her belly, hair tickling the outer edge of her ribcage. 'What you doin'?'

Wishing that things didn't have to end so abruptly. But the comfort of knowing it was only one perfect night meant she didn't have to expend any more energy on it. She was done and dusted with her Jack infatuation. He could go home and she could carry on concentrating on her business plan with a lovely memory and an unbroken heart.

He nuzzled again. The smell of them wafted through the air. The smell of him clung to her. She wanted to preserve it somehow. To preserve this moment, last night, yesterday.

So, okay, maybe the Jack infatuation was lingering a little. It had been insanely sexy. Insanely glorious.

Insane.

To even think of sleeping with him was a crazy notion, but now she had to deal with the aftermath. Head-on seemed the best way to go. 'For the record, just so you know, it's not my fault I'm late today. This time, you are to blame, buster. I'm getting up; I have to get my stall organised right now before someone else gets my spot.'

His head lifted from the pillow lazily. 'Would they dare?'

'Yes. We are given a permit and allocated a site, but everyone vies for prime spots. If I don't get there soon I'll miss it.'

His head hit the pillow again. 'What time is it?'

'Six forty-five.'

'And it's a bank holiday? What about the lie-in?' Rubbing his face and yawning, he looked so right in her bed, his dark skin against the cream linen duvet cover, mussed-up hair against the headboard.

Then suddenly the full impact of what they'd done seemed to settle on him as he looked around the room at the discarded clothes and dishevelled bed. And it didn't sit easily. He might have looked right for the room, but he'd started to look a little out of sorts with the scenario.

'Hello? Mr Time Obsession, where have you gone? It's a work day for me; I don't get bank holidays or weekends. This is how it is—odd hours, odd clients.' She dug a finger into his ribs and watched him smother a smile. 'You can stay here while I get organised if you don't want to get up yet, although you'll have to leave when I do. I don't like people being here when I'm not.' She didn't need to explain why.

'Do you need me…to…er…help out again?' The tone sounded hopeful that she'd say no and let them both off the hook.

They had to go back to their normal lives. Although now she was changed a little. Still frazzled—check. Disorganised—check. Craving his touch—that hadn't been there before. And he could go back to being a grumpy control freak important media man. Their paths would cross at a quirky Irish wedding in a week or two's time, and then nothing. That's what they both wanted. They'd agreed.

But she doubted anything could be as sensual or beautiful as last night. Anything or any man. She forced a smile. 'No, thanks, you get off home. I can manage fine on my own.'

He was halfway off the bed now, grabbing at his jeans on the floor. He couldn't have been more obvious about his need to leave, and his regret about the night they'd shared—that was written in the shadows under his eyes and the stiff taut jaw. 'Okay, if you're sure. It's just that I have work to do as well. Editing for a project. A deadline. I should probably…'

'Relax. Don't worry; I'm not some rabid crazy woman.' At his raised eyebrow, she corrected herself. 'Okay, so I am a crazy woman. But I'm not holding you to anything past last night. It was fun, though. Margaritas, dancing... and, well, you blew my socks off. It was great, but...' Was she rabbiting? Protesting too much? Convincing herself?

But she needed to properly take control of something— really take control, not like last night, which had been a playful battle of wills and heaps of sex-tastic fun. But she got the feeling that if she left it up to him he'd be jumped up and gone and no word said at all. And she didn't want to be waiting for him, to hold out for a phone call or some kind of meeting that would be all shades of awkward. She needed it clear-cut and finished so she could put him neatly into her mental spreadsheet of fantastic one-nighters. And nowhere near the one that said maybe...perhaps...if only. That was, after all, if she'd had any idea of how to con- jure up a spreadsheet in the first place. Plus, he'd be the only one on it.

She was getting in too deep and that was the way to disaster. She couldn't afford to stuff up again; her head couldn't take it and her heart certainly couldn't.

To say he looked relieved would be an understatement. 'Yeah. Yeah, it was...'

Was what? Fun? Great? Stupid. Slinking off the bed, she pulled on a dressing gown, suddenly embarrassed about being naked in front of him. Bad enough he'd see her with no clothes on, but emotionally exposed? Never. 'So, if you'll excuse me, I'll just get a shower and then start packing things up.'

Wrestling his T-shirt over those big broad shoulders, he paused. 'You're sure you don't need a hand?'

'No, Jack. I worked out how to use showers a long time

ago. I'll manage just fine.' Then she closed the door and
prayed he'd be gone by the time she'd towelled off.

'Okay, so we need to find a focus for the narrative here.
There's no point just showing a bunch of shots from artistic
angles; we need something more meaty and meaningful.'

Three days down and Jack still wasn't sure this editor
had any idea how to actually edit. To be fair, he was new
to the Zoom team and still learning the ropes, but Jack had
chosen him because of his great credentials. They were
getting precisely nowhere. Nothing was hanging together,
and the continued success of Zoom depended on everything gelling and hitting the weekend deadline. He tried
to haul some oxygen into his lungs but the cutting room
was tiny and airless and the walls seemed to be closing in.

That was what lack of sleep did: played hell with his
concentration. Three double shots of caffeine hadn't done
their usual trick.

He stuck his feet up on the console and tried a different
approach. 'Look, my vision here is that this is a chance to
let Jono tell his own story through showing his contradic-
tions, show he's human. He doesn't say what he means,
but his body language is a real tell. See here, how he tells
her he doesn't want the baby?' Jack rewound the footage,
knowing he was overstepping the mark a little. Producers
rarely called the shots in the editing suite, but everyone at
Zoom knew he was more hands-on than most. Billy would
just have to get to know his quirks. 'Here. Look at his
face when she storms out of the room. Pure devastation.
Then, we later find out about his first wife's late miscar-
riage. That is pure gold. If we can juxtapose those pieces
together it'll make great TV.'

'Sure.' Billy shot him a look that said: *get the hell out*

of my cutting room. 'Whatever you want, boss. Whatever you want.'

Yeah. Great point, mate. What did he want? That was as muddled as this documentary segment was.

The other night he'd been pretty damned clear about it. At least his libido had been. He'd wanted Cassie so much he'd actually felt a physical ache.

But now? He felt as if he'd been sucker-punched by one of the street kids he'd tried to fight off all those years ago. And just as helpless too. Cassie was beautiful, sensual, funny. Once upon a time he could have listed every one of her attributes but then countered them all with rationality: the effect on him was purely physical. He could walk away any time from that kind of attraction and not break into a sweat.

But it had been an all-out struggle to leave her on Monday morning. Until she'd all but pushed him out of bed and sent him on his way. Clearly, she had no trouble with the one-night scenario. Which bothered him more than it should.

Thoughts of her in the shower kept flickering through his mind. Half of him—most of him—seemed to be on the verge of running back to her apartment and taking up where they'd left off.

Never had a woman had that kind of effect on him before. Never had he forged a connection with someone that was so strong, so elemental that he'd wanted to stay in bed with her instead of going to work. Never had he allowed anyone to distract him so utterly from his career, his production company. His one constant. The only thing he had to be proud of, to show those non-believers that he was worth something after all.

Everything he'd worked for was at risk here—because of a woman. Because of a connection. He knew better than that, but he just couldn't shake her out of his head. Sitting here achieving diddly-squat wasn't helping. He needed air. 'You know what, Billy? This isn't happening today. Let's give it up and start again fresh tomorrow. What do you say?'

Billy nodded and almost dashed out of the door. Had he been that much of a pain in the ass to work with? 'Okay, man. Get some sleep, eh? Chillax.'

'Yeah. Thanks.' He didn't know how, except to lose himself inside a beautiful chef. But clearly that was strictly off the menu. He needed a long cold shower. An early night. And some kind of mind-erasing drug before he set foot in work again.

An hour later, he was running up the steps to his house and discovered a small white cardboard box outside his door. His name was scrawled on the lid. Inside, he discovered a note and a sort of doughnut-shaped cake that smelt exactly like Cassie's kitchen. Her bedroom. Her. His groin tightened instinctively at the thought—she was driving him steadily mad. Being with her. Not being with her. Either way, he was doomed and his work was shot. Either way, she hadn't lingered long enough to see him when she'd dropped this off.

He peered at the note.

I never really said thanks for helping me out with the stall the other day, so THANK YOU. I'm playing around with the recipe for these—all the rage at the moment. I needed a guinea pig and thought of you. ;-) Let me know what you think. C.

Five minutes later, he was licking vanilla sugar from his fingers then stabbing her number into his mobile. It would be rude not to show gratitude at the very least. 'Hey. Thanks for the cake.'

'My pleasure. You like?' She sounded tired but relaxed. If there was any kind of tension about talking to him she wasn't showing it.

His heart-rate settled to the jiggly tempo it had whenever she was on his mind. Half excited, half comfortable. 'It was perfect. Kind of like a doughnut, but like a croissant too.'

'Ten out of ten; I'll make a commis chef out of you yet. It's a croissant dough shaped and deep-fried like a doughnut—and that runny stuff in the middle? Confectioners' custard—I love that stuff. My, my, what excellent observation skills you have.'

'All the better to devour...your cooking.' His stomach groaned and once again he realised he'd gone a day without eating. And three days without seeing her. That he even knew that set alarms off again. He ignored them. 'Is there anything else I can be your guinea pig for?'

He heard the laughter in her throat. Thoughts of her straddling him, head thrown back and laughing made him hard. Very hard. Her voice lowered a little. 'Why, Jack? What do you have in mind?'

Apart from phone sex? Any kind of sex? Sex tended to be way better when the two people having it were in the same room.

Whoa. He knew the agenda. There was nothing between them except a mutual lust and he'd managed to get to twenty-eight without getting carried away by that particular boat. He could control this. 'I haven't had dinner yet. You?'

'No. I've just finished a job so I have some leftovers to look forward to.'

'Enough for two?' The tension he'd missed earlier?

There it was in the sharp intake of breath, the pause, the garbled answer.

'Er...I have...well, I guess that would... You want to share?'

'Is barbecuing corn involved? Because I can do without that.'

'No. But there's a couple of steaks and a chimichurri sauce, pan-fried potatoes with rosemary. Caramelised nectarines—' her voice definitely caught a little '—but it's just food, Jack. Nothing else.'

He found his keys faster than Houdini. 'Okay, I'll come over.'

'No. Wait. I'll come to you.'

'Oh. Okay, your call.' How many times had he done that? Gone over to a woman's house instead of inviting them over, just so he could control how long he stayed and get out quick if things got heavy? 'You mean, so you get to choose when to leave.'

'*Exactement*, my friend. *Exactement*. Plus, it's about time I got to see how the other half live. I'll be there in twenty.'

And that was the moment he could have said this was not a good idea, but she'd hung up before he got the chance.

Twenty minutes later she was at the door, fresh-faced and dressed in a yellow and black polka dot wide-brimmed floppy sun hat, pink strappy top and red flouncy skirt, laden down with plastic boxes and a bottle of expensive French red. Her hair hung loose round her shoulders in big looping curls and he fought the urge to nuzzle right in and inhale.

'Hi, Jack.'

'Hey. Right on time.'

'I'm getting better.' Shoving the food into his arms, she

took a deep breath, waiting until he was looking right at her. 'Jack, just so we're clear, this doesn't—'

'Mean anything? I know. I know. It's just food. Come in.' He moved back to let her in, his gut clenching at the thought of having her here and not having her. But he could do this—he just had to concentrate hard on not looking at her smile, her hair. Or listening too intently to the light laugh blowing through his humid house like fresh air.

Stepping into the lounge, her mouth opened wide. 'Wow. Some place you have here. Have you just moved in?'

'No. Been here five years. First place I bought when I'd got enough for a mortgage down payment.' Winning an industry award had helped bring the big guns knocking at Zoom's door and, for some reason, he just couldn't bring himself to move out of the neighbourhood he'd grown used to. Time was he'd have given anything to leave the place, but he'd been drawn back here with a feeling of needing some familiarity. God knew why. Guess it was also close to Lizzie.

And now close to Cassie. Luck? Fate? Chance? Whatever. It didn't mean anything.

'Oh, really—five years?' Her eyes widened now as she ran a hand across the back of his sofa. 'It needs a little colour, Jack. You have heard of colour, haven't you? It's like…you know, that soft tickly stuff on the ground in Holland Park? Grass? That's green. That big bright circle in the sky? Sun. That's yellow.'

'Yes, well, we don't all need to live in Willy Wonka land. I like things to be tidy and ordered.'

'You don't say.'

He looked at his place—stark and spacious and white. All white. Sofa, chairs, rug, blinds. Easy to match, the designer had told him. As if he cared; he wasn't trying for *Homes and Gardens* home of the month. Home wasn't something he knew much about, having not really had one since he was six years old. Hell, for ever, in fact. He shrugged, far more interested in the riot of colour standing in the middle of the room. She swirled around, her skirt kicking out in a circle, revealing legs that he preferred wrapped around him than pirouetting, and leaving her scent everywhere. *Everywhere*. His chest became a crushing mass of emotion, the most prominent in there being lust. But there was more. Just…more. 'Home decor isn't top of my to-do list. I just need a bed, a kettle and somewhere to keep my stuff. I'm hardly ever here.'

'Clearly. It barely looks lived in.' She shook her head. 'I have a sudden urge to mess everything up. Unstraighten the rug. Half close the blinds—at a jaunty angle. Run dirty footprints across the floor. Something. Where are the knick-knacks? Photos?'

'Of what?'

'Family? Lizzie? You? Your pet iguana?'

'I'm very sorry, but truth is I don't have one.' Family, or iguana.

'What a shame. And I was holding out all this time just to meet him.' Her mouth formed a perfect pout as she threw her hat, like a Frisbee, onto the sofa, where it sat messily, out of place, like a big bright stain against the alabaster fabric. 'Maybe you should get one and brighten the place up a bit—or wouldn't the green scales go with the decor? How about a pet that's white? A cockatoo?'

'And have someone else in here endlessly chattering away too? No, thank you.'

She laughed, lowering her voice to a comedy whisper. 'Oh, well, we'd better move into another room. Quick. I'd be afraid to spill anything and ruin the look. All that red wine, green sauce, golden potatoes. Shudder.' But she flicked a sarcastic look towards her hat and grinned.

She followed him through to the kitchen and started opening drawers, ferreting in cupboards, lifting out plates and pans, working her way round as if she'd designed the damned place. It looked as if she wouldn't be happy until every darned thing he owned was piled on to the counters. There was a hum in her throat, though—no denying that the moment she walked into a kitchen she was in her happy zone. Nudging a drawer closed with a swing of her left hip, she handed him the wine bottle. 'You get this poured and I'll sort the food. So, how's the week been?'

'Frustrating. A hot sense of running round in circles and not getting where I wanted to be.' Kind of like right now, but he had wanted to sack Billy, not rip his clothes off. 'Yours?'

'Okay, I guess. I scored another couple of jobs, which is good. Word of mouth really helps in this business. The mother of the head injury girl recommended me to a couple of her friends. More kiddies' parties, but that in turn may lead to something else. Plus, I managed to negotiate a better rate with the bank for paying my debt off. So I'm pretty happy.'

'Excellent. Well done. So we have cause to celebrate?' He handed her a glass of wine and chinked his against it. She gave him a full-blown mesmerising smile that whipped the air from his lungs. 'One day you'll land a mega contract and things will be sweet for Sweet Treats. Pardon the pun.'

'Oh, so funny. Big contracts are hard to find and even harder to win. But I'll take any good stuff that comes along. What's been your problem?'

He told her about Billy and his less than stellar editing skills; for some reason, offloading to her made him feel better. Which was weird because the running of Zoom was his alone and he'd liked that, liked the autonomy, calling all the shots. Usually. 'What I can't understand is how he had such great references and yet he's not shaping up.'

'Maybe it's you being there that makes him nervous?'

He laughed. 'Oh, yeah, that'd be right. Blame the boss.'

She stopped stirring and waved the wooden spoon in his direction. 'Absolutely. First rule of the kitchen: the head chef is always in charge and therefore always to blame. If not him, then the restaurant owner. Never the minions. Isn't it the same in your line of work?'

He didn't need to go into the hierarchy of the film business—safe to say, editors were just as respected as the directors. 'There's probably a whole load of dissent behind my back. Why am I not surprised you have authority issues?'

'Why am I not surprised you have subordinate issues? Get off his back; give the guy a chance to prove himself.' She pigged her eyes at him. 'Stay out of the cutting room.'

'Whoa. Radical—not sure if I can do that.'

'Of course you can. Try it—stay away for a couple of days and let him get on with it. Take a chill pill. Control freak.' Flicking the frying pan away from her, she flipped the almost perfect squares of flecked potatoes in hot oil until they began to sizzle and a fragrant garlic and rosemary scent filled the air. All around her was debris, discarded pots, oil smears on the granite. Thick slabs of bloody steak oozing onto a plate.

He picked up the plate. 'Mess freak. Here, give me that meat.'

'Oh, no. You are not going to set fire to my Wagyu like you did those corn cobs. You can't cook, remember?'

'I can do man food. Give it here.' Not giving her any more opportunity to resist, he took the steaks and placed them on a hot griddle pan, where they immediately began to sizzle. After a couple of minutes he turned them over and noted that so far they were cooking to perfection. *Gotcha.* 'I want to cook at least one thing for you.'

'Thanks. That's actually very nice. See, you can be if you try.' Cassie leaned against him as she checked out the progress. Her hair tickled against his chin and he pressed a small kiss on to the top of her head. It just happened, instinctively, before he could catch himself.

Unsure of what her response might be, he stepped back a little. For a few seconds she looked up at him, as if weighing him up, as if working something out, tension spiralling until he just wanted her to say some damn thing.

But then she gave his backside a quick squeeze and grinned up at him. He let out a breath. Man, this felt so unlike anything he'd had before. A sort of comfortable excitement. There was that word again. Comfortable. He knew better than that. Needed to be on his guard.

And yet he was a man now, not an angry, confused teenager. Not a six-year-old, eight-year-old. Ten. He knew not to expect anything to last. Not to invest every last bit of himself in something doomed to end. This time he was definitely in control of things. He could walk away from Cassie any time—but having a little fun didn't mean anything. It didn't mean anything at all.

She watched as he checked the underside of the meat. 'Good job. Good job. You're getting very handy in here.'

'Not as much as I'd like,' he growled. His left hand curved around her bottom. Excitement won over comfort and pinged across his belly and arrowed south, to his groin, his legs, then back up to the top of his head. 'I'm just going to leave this to…rest?'

'Excellent. Well, everything else is ready so I'll quickly prepare the dessert while we're waiting.' Twisting off the top of a bottle of rum, she slugged a good amount into a pan and then a small amount into two shot glasses. 'Got to test it first to make sure it's okay.' She winked and handed him a glass, then downed her drink in one gulp, shuddered as it hit her throat. 'Wow. That'll do. Your turn.'

Her eyes brightened as he followed suit, laughed as he flinched and wiped his mouth with the back of his hand. 'It's okay, I guess.'

'That is a quality product. It's better than okay.' Then she added butter and some runny honey to the pan and stirred until it was thick and hot and well mixed. 'Now, the next taste test. I love this stuff.'

She put her finger in the pan and pulled it out covered in thick golden sauce.

Before it reached her mouth he grabbed her hand and slowly sucked the sauce from her finger. It tasted soft and sweet and warm, like Caribbean nights, summer days.

He saw the moment her eyes misted, the second desire softened her, the way she pressed against the counter, the momentary flicker of her eyes as she registered that he wanted her again. That he had not stopped wanting her. That she wanted him too. *'Jack.'*

'It tastes very good indeed, but I think we need to try it again, just to make sure.' His mouth went dry and wet at the same time at the anticipation of tasting her. Then, he put his finger in the sauce and offered it to her. When her lips clamped around his finger and she slid her hot wet mouth over his skin he was gone. No amount of self-control would keep him from having her. He dipped his head to her mouth and sucked her tongue. Nipped her lip. Grazed her throat, her neck.

'Delicious.' Again, he put his finger in the sauce and trailed it from the pulse in her throat to the 'v' of her breasts. Followed the trail with his tongue, spurred on by the guttural moans in her throat. She leaned against the counter and he crushed her against it, tearing her top to one side, fitting his hand inside her bra and palming her breast.

'My turn now. Don't want it to go to waste.' This time she put three fingers in the sauce and wiped them over his cheek. Then she opened her mouth and licked it off, her gaze fixed on his, her eyes glittering with need. Button by button, she undid his shirt and let it drop, then she pressed a sticky kiss to each of his nipples. More sauce. More kisses. Then she was pulling at his belt and undoing his zip.

'Come here.' Part growl, part desperation. Walking her to the table, he leaned her back against it, dragged her skirt up and looked at her creamy skin, those thighs parted for him, the flimsy scrap of lace that was the only barrier between now and heaven.

Who the hell was this woman with such a hold over him? Who he wanted to please, wanted to satisfy, wanted to hear his name on her lips, whose name he said again and again in his dreams. What the hell was happening to him? God knew. He was past thinking, past rationalising. He tried to control his breathing, his need, but his brains had all gone south. No—there was something else, a feeling. Something confusing and yet so very clear—just there. Something he didn't understand, that he didn't want to understand.

There was nothing to do but to show her what he wanted, how he felt. And even if he couldn't work it out for himself then his body definitely knew.

Cassie felt him stretch her, inside her, filling her, and the rush of need for him intensified. His gaze so intense, his face so beautiful. *This wasn't going to happen.* But how the hell could she stop it?

When he sucked on her nipple she cried out, when he called her name with such ferocity she came, so hard and fast it felt as if she was spiralling out of her consciousness. Then, when he cupped her face in his hands and kissed her so tenderly, she almost cried with the absolute purity of this achingly precious thing they had found. This connection that made her feel safe and happy and yet free at the same time.

He kissed her again, as if his life depended on it. As if he too felt it but didn't understand. It was so right. So beautiful.

Yes. *This*. She'd been lying to herself when she arrived on his doorstep. When she'd brought the cake round earlier. When he'd kissed her, when he made love to her.

It did mean something. It meant everything.

She arched her back as he thrust faster and faster, wanting more. Wanting more. Wanting more...

And she knew that she couldn't stop wanting this, wanting him. Knew that a part of her could never recover from knowing him—that, no matter how much she tried to prevent herself falling for him, or protect her heart against yet another man who might not care as much for her, a part of her would forever belong to Jack.

CHAPTER ELEVEN

MINUTES LATER, CASSIE shifted, her back hurting now against the hard table, the stars in her peripheral vision slowly dissipating and the sticky residue pulling at her skin. But, as soon as she moved, Jack's arms were around her, pulling her up, laughing. 'Whoa, well, that's the hors d'oeuvres over with.'

'Can't wait for the main course, then. And dessert...I'm looking forward to that.' She kissed his chest and straightened her clothes, the turn of events and the way she so easily fell back into his arms a little shocking. The meat sat on the counter, going cold. 'Hmm, what to do with the steak now?'

Jack zipped up, washed his hands and looked ready for more cooking action. 'Microwave it?'

'Heathen. Get out of my kitchen now.'

Trapping her against the bench again he playfully kissed her nose, head, throat. 'Er...it's my kitchen and I get to say what goes on here.'

'And that's quite a lot, judging by the last half hour.'

He grinned. 'Again, not as much as I'd like.'

After she'd reheated the meat—on the griddle—and dinner had been eaten, Cassie excused herself to go to the bathroom. She knew you could tell a lot about a man by his choice of toiletries, the cleanliness of his space, which she was suitably impressed by. Not quite the OCD perfect line-up of bottles she'd expected; in fact, a happy mess. His towels were soft and warm, hanging neatly on the rail. So far, so normal. Except...

'Why do you keep your BAFTA award on a shelf in the bathroom?' she asked him as they started to clear away the dinner plates. 'I mean, I've heard of people doing that, but I didn't actually believe it.'

He shrugged. 'To be honest, it was the first place I put it when I came back from the ceremony and I've had no reason to move it. Where else am I supposed to keep it? It seems as good a place as any.'

'I don't know, but I'd be shouting it from the rooftops. A big banner outside saying: award here!'

'Who am I going to shout it to? Everyone at work knows I got it. My friends do.'

'But it's such an amazing achievement. You must be so proud.'

Clearly reluctant to talk about himself any more, he looked out of the kitchen window into the garden; it was a warm late summer evening. 'We should have eaten outside while we can. Do you want to go for a walk in the park? It's lovely this time of day, and not so busy.'

'Yes, why not? Work up an appetite for dessert.' Although, if the hors d'oeuvres were anything to go by, she was already hungry for more. 'I'll have to make more sauce. A lot more.' She winked at him and started to make her way to the front door.

'No. This way.' He led her out through the narrow back garden, under a bower of blossoming white flowers, through a large gate and into the manicured gardens of Holland Park. Before them stretched a long tree-lined path, awash with dappled sunlight. Just across the way she saw the flickering flags of various embassies, and into some of the higher windows above towering walls and barbed wire.

'Wow, this is brilliant. I've often walked through here and wondered about the kind of people who lived in these houses bordering the park. And now I know.'

'Oh, yes? What exactly do you know? I'm only in a small house compared to one of those mansions. And what you see is what you get with me, I'm afraid.'

No, there was so much more to him than he wanted to tell her. So much he was hiding from, or running from; she didn't quite know. So much that probably meant the difference between him staying and going. Things working or not even given a chance.

A tight fist of pain under her ribcage stalled her breath at that thought.

She wasn't ready for this to end; it was too irresistible, too new. With a shock, she realised she wanted something more with Jack—something that this fledgling connection could build on. Because she wasn't ready to let him go; she wasn't ready to walk away. Sure, they were complete opposites on most levels, but they were the same when they made love, the same when they kissed, the same when they talked and laughed.

She wanted more. Despite everything. Her stomach curled into a knot.

After everything she'd tried to prevent, those times she'd fought her feelings, those times she'd slammed up barriers—but even now she couldn't think of having more days without him, like the last three, wondering if she was in too deep or not deep enough. Wondering if they could make something precious together or not. She was through with being scared, of slamming up walls.

But she knew too that telling him would be insane.

He took her hand and they strolled towards the

Orangery rose gardens and sparkling fountains. She remembered catering a wedding here not long ago, the happy
openness of the bride and groom, who had talked her leg
off about their hopes and plans; the feeling that she'd never
found that with any man. Did she push too hard or not
enough? Or just choose the wrong men in the end? But
Jack was…well, he was different to any man she knew.

'Okay, well, I know you're a control maestro.'

'With you around, it's good to inject a little order or the
world would implode.' He squeezed her hand.

'I know you work hard and play reluctantly. But when
you do allow yourself to have fun you really enjoy it. That
you're wicked at sex.' That got a press against a tree and a
long leisurely kiss that pushed away any kind of thought
process at all. When she pulled away she could barely remember how to speak. She kept a hold of him because
she'd almost forgotten how to stand upright too. 'Is sex in
a public place a crime?'

He thought for a moment and sucked air through his
teeth. 'Sadly, I think so.'

'Damn. Wow. Okay. Right.' She tried a step forward on
liquid legs. Seemed just about okay. But better hold on to
him just in case. 'Where was I?'

'I'm a sex God or something.' He pulled her against
him and laughed.

She loved the way he looked when he laughed—so
liberated and carefree and downright gorgeous. And it
seemed to be happening more and more and she just knew
part of that was because of her. Pride slid into the mix of
emotions swirling in her gut. 'Oh, yes, I remember now,
you're a woeful cook but a quick learner. You have an
amazing talent but, for some very bizarre reason, you are
reluctant to celebrate it. You love your sister. And, apart
from that, I don't know much else.'

'Good God, woman, isn't that enough?' But he must have known it wasn't, could never be, not after everything they'd shared. Beside her, she felt his body stiffen slightly. 'What do you want to know?'

'I don't know.' So she was going to push a little, then back off if it felt like too much. 'There's something I've been wondering about. You once said you moved a lot— Lizzie mentioned you were shifted to someone's house? Mrs Something... When she baked the cake with the melted icing? And you cut her off mid-sentence. Why?'

He dropped her hand and for a moment she thought he was going to walk away, but he didn't. 'You don't want to hear about my old history.'

'Actually, I do.' She sat down on the lawn and tugged him next to her.

He tried to pull away. 'It's getting late.'

'Jack, I know I'm walking a thin line here. I know there are no promises or roses for us. But...oh, God, this is too hard.' She climbed to her knees, knowing he was used to being on his own, that he liked it. That he had never tried to open up to her. Time to get out. This was stupid. 'Forget it.'

His gaze locked on to hers, his mouth a thin line of uncertainty, and she saw a battle raging deep inside him.

After a few moments he sat on the grass and wrapped his arms round his legs, creating his own cocoon, rested his chin on his knees. Again he asked, 'What do you want to know? Because there's a whole lot of stuff there and I don't know where to begin. I never know where to begin.'

A silence wove around them as she watched him, huddled and sitting apart from her, her heart breaking just a little at the darkness in his eyes. Hurt? Because of her or because of some memory she was insisting he relive just so she could feel closer to him? 'I'm sorry, Jack.'

'Nothing to be sorry about,' he murmured, his voice

barely audible. But neither of them got up to go. The last dying rays of the sun warmed her face but she felt cold because she had a feeling that whatever he was going to say wasn't pretty. Where exactly to begin? In the end she just plainly asked, 'Why did you pin up Lizzie's hair?'

He squeezed his eyes closed. 'Because I was the only one who she'd allow anywhere near her hair. It's a bit wild and used to get into knots which took forever to comb through. Besides, no one else had the time. Or inclination.'

'Why not?'

He turned away, as if deciding what to say. When he turned back to her, his face was serious, that lovely deep mellow voice had lost all emotion. Cold, matter-of-fact, causing a chill down the back of her neck. 'We weren't part of anyone's lives for long. No one was really interested in what yet more foster kids wanted. So it was down to me. I looked out for her, looked after her as best I could. You ever need nit removal, I'm your go-to guy.' He tried to find a smile, but failed and looked even more drawn because of it.

'God, that's awful.' Cassie remembered her sisters fighting over who would plait her hair—over and over again. For a good part of her life she'd been their plaything, a living doll that they'd dressed and fed and pushed around in a baby buggy even when she was far too big to fit in it. When their father had died they'd closed ranks and protected her, shielded her from the emotional upheaval as much as they could. Even now, she was treated as if she wasn't quite grown-up, and it was annoying, but she couldn't imagine having no one interested in her. Heartbreaking. But it explained something about the way he felt he could barge into his sister's wedding. They must have grown close if they'd only had each other.

Only each other. Her throat closed over.

He shrugged, but he couldn't hide the resentment. The tinge of sadness playing out as smudges under his eyes. 'Yeah, well, you can forget the puppy-eyed pity, Cassie. It's life. And forever ago. If I went anywhere near Lizzie's hair now she'd probably hit me with a solid right hook.'

She tried to laugh, but her throat was too raw; there was no humour here. None. 'Why were you fostered?'

Again, a pause. A look away. A battle for words. 'Marion, our mother, wasn't mother material. She was poor and uneducated and didn't know how to look after babies—but she sure knew how to make them. Lizzie and I don't have the same dad, but that's fairly obvious. I'm not sure if Marion knew who our dads were—difficult to know when you're having regular sex with lots of guys for cash.'

'She was a prostitute?' She tried not to be judgemental, but the hopelessness of the situation bit deep in her heart.

'Yes. But it was a means to an end, and meant she had no time or energy—or love, really—for us. We were just mouths to feed that she didn't want. I spent six years starving and dirty, trying to look after Lizzie when I had no clue how, barely more than a baby myself. One day I told my teacher the extent of what was happening at home and she called the authorities. Then we were moved, and moved, and moved.'

'Why? Why didn't someone take you in and love you?'

He shook his head and laughed, coldly. 'What a nice rosy picture of the foster system you have. One family moved back to Australia and didn't want to take us with them. One mum got sick and couldn't look after us. Another *mum* got pregnant and had her own baby and we were suddenly surplus to her requirements.'

'That's cruel, Jack. Do you ever have any contact with Marion? Know where she is? Is she still alive?'

He nodded. 'As part of the deal, she was supposed to

stay in contact with us—supervised access with a social worker. She never turned up. Not once. At first it was gutting. Then it was expected. Then it was normal. We tried to forget her and look forward. So every time we started at a new place we thought: *this is going to be it*, our home. We unpacked our pathetic grubby suitcases and got excited and dreamt big, tried to fit in, tried to make new friends, tried to be the perfect kids just so they'd keep us. And every single time they swooped in and took us away; the last place we stayed was a grubby children's home. By then we'd stopped dreaming, stopped getting excited, stopped trying to connect with anyone but each other.'

She reached over to him and wrapped her hand over his. When he took it she shuffled closer and leaned against him to give him some physical contact, because she didn't want him having to face saying all this on his own. He had her now too and she was a damned good fighter. 'So you relied solely on each other. I feel bad that I accused you of being overbearing and overprotective.'

'Don't, for God's sake. You're coming from a very different scenario. Your father died in tragic circumstances; your family had a way of dealing with it. And you're more than entitled to bitch a little.'

'But still, I shouldn't have been so damning of the way you were acting.'

'You were right, though. I was over the top, barging in.' He rubbed the back of his neck and spoke to his feet. 'See, I did the best I could, but Lizzie was damaged by it. When I found her that day I felt responsible. I knew she wasn't well, and I'd left her alone. She nearly died. I decided I'd have to do a damned sight better for us or lie down and die alongside her. The only thing I was good at was making amateur films so, once she got a little better, I threw all my energy into that, earning cash to pay for her rent and college fees. Only it takes me away more than I want. Not that it matters so much now she has Callum.'

'Yes, but she'll always need her brother.' She squeezed his arm.

'Yeah.' But he didn't look convinced. He wanted his sister to be happy, but he wanted to be part of her life too, that was clear. And Lizzie had needed him so much over the years, but now she had another man to love.

'Seriously, Jack, you may be a giant pain in the backside, but she'll always love you.' That raised a smile and she put her arm round his shoulder. In one sweep he had her in his arms, holding her. Just holding.

Cassie didn't think it was possible to feel more for the man than she already did. That he'd come through such a childhood and been so successful and wholly sane astounded her. Impressed her. She felt nothing but admiration for what he'd achieved. And a whole lot else. Her heart swelled at how much he'd grown and moved on, how hard he'd fought. How this kind and gentle man who had enough demons of his own had managed to protect his sister.

Not only that, but he was everything she'd described to him before. He was considerate, had looked after her when she'd been sick, had helped her out on her stall, had ridden the waves of her continual lateness and still offered her the contract for his sister's wedding. He made her feel safe, wanted, sexy. She hoped more than anything that she instilled those things in him; she wanted to make him smile every day. Every minute. Wanted him with such a need she couldn't think straight, couldn't sleep.

If that was love, then perhaps, just perhaps she was falling in love with him.

But the harsh truth was that he wasn't in love with her. This whole fling thing didn't mean anything, they'd agreed. And yet, even so, she'd done the most stupid thing in the world and thought she could control her emotions.

Her throat felt raw. No, her whole chest was constricted. She could not love this man. *You do not want to get involved with me.*

This was the worst possible thing to happen, the worst timing. The worst man to fall for—one who didn't just not love her, but who didn't *want* to love anyone. He'd spent his life making sure he didn't fall prey, like she had, to something that might damage him. He'd been damaged enough. *I'm not going to open every wound for you.*

He'd warned her and she had not listened. She leaned her head against his shoulder as he stroked her back in long soft movements. Breathed in his so familiar smell, felt the tension melt away from his body. Holding him, just touching him was torture and ecstasy. She didn't want to let go, but she had to. Like tearing away a layer of her heart, bloody and bruised.

Was it worse then, to never allow yourself to fall in love for risk of hurting too much? Or to fall in love anyway and endure the hurt that came at the end?

She wanted to make him feel better, somehow, but declaring how she felt would surely make him run in the opposite direction. Selfish, really, to have heard his story and think about how this might affect her, but self-protection ran deep through her blood too. She twisted from him and looked at her watch, keeping her voice gentle. 'Goodness, it's getting late. We should get going.'

'Yeah. I guess.' He huffed out a long breath, closing his eyes. He didn't move. Just sat there for a few more minutes and as she watched him she knew she couldn't let this chance go. It was rash and dangerous, but wasn't that the way she lived her life? Rattling out of control?

He looked so desolate and alone that if she did tell him

how she felt then maybe she could change things for him, prove to him that good things could happen, that people could be treasured and wanted. That you could find happiness, a home—it was possible.

Maybe they could work things out?

Maybe not. Maybe she was on a hiding to nothing. He'd laugh at her.

Like him, she'd been fighting her feelings for so long, scared to trust anyone ever again, scared of them taking over, of losing herself. But with Jack she was still complete—she didn't lose anything of herself, but she gained so much more.

Could she? Dare she? Take a risk? Like he'd done that first day he'd walked up the steps to kiss her. Or the second time when he'd turned up at her house. Or the time he'd helped her with her tyre and then still given her the catering contract. For someone in control, he'd taken a few risks around her.

Knowing he was prepared to do that for her had made her stronger, made her start to trust again.

If she broached the subject, maybe they could move past this barrier of pretence they'd erected, stop making out that this was a temporary attraction, that after the wedding they could walk away unscathed. Because this turning up on each other's doorstep, the fevered love-making, the shared jokes…wasn't that worth something? She damned well thought it was.

Her heart thundered, she couldn't walk, couldn't stop this. Maybe it was time to be honest.

Jack stood and took hold of Cassie's hand again—things felt better that way. And, yeah, although his gut felt hollowed out a little, he was still whole. Kind of more whole now than he'd ever been. Sharing that stuff was hard; it made him remember things he didn't want to ever relive. And he'd worried how she would take it. It wasn't exactly a fairy tale, but they were past that, he knew. Neither of them believed in all that guff about happy ever afters. Cassie was a realist, he'd come to learn.

But she seemed in a hurry to get back to the house. Maybe his story had shocked her more than he'd expected it would but he wasn't ready to go back inside; he liked being free, breathing in fresh air. 'We could just walk over to the Japanese garden, then double back to the house?'

'No, can we just go straight back?' She looked a little shaken but she didn't let go of his hand.

'Hey, are you okay?'

'Yes, thanks.'

'I didn't mean to upset you. It doesn't affect me any more; it's just what happened.' *Liar.*

He was so used to her amazing genuine sunny smiles that he knew this one was half pretence, half something else. Sadness? Pity? Her voice sounded strained and strange. 'I'm not upset, Jack. Well, I mean, what happened to you was very upsetting, but I'm just tired. Too much excitement for one day.'

'Again, not as much as I'd like.' It was becoming a running joke. He slipped his arm round her waist and pulled her closer, running fingers across an inch of bare skin between her top and skirt waistband and he thought about breaking every rule and having her here on the path.

Did she flinch? Or had he tickled her? He couldn't be sure but she seemed disconcerted, different. Serious. Perhaps she would smile again at the thought of some more fun. Clear the air. Freshen things up again. 'Are you ready for dessert? And…do you want to stay over?'

That was a biggie for them both; last time she'd sent him packing, this time he'd make sure she wanted to stay again. She seemed startled, her eyes lighting up. 'Oh. I… yes. But there's something you need to know.'

'That you snore? No worries, I have industry standard ear plugs.'

She laughed nervously, her hand became fidgety and he let it loose so she could talk with it. But she walked along, her head down, the crazy mess of colours of her clothes blending in with the summer flowers that flanked the path. Her body seemed quieted, still almost. Eerily composed. This not talking was so unlike her. They walked in silence for a while as dusk cast russet shades through the trees.

When they reached his gate she rested her hand on the lever but didn't open it. She seemed to be struggling with something in her head, then finally she looked as if she'd decided what to say and how to say it. 'Jack. I need to tell you something.'

Her face was so serious his stomach twisted into a knot. *She's not catering the wedding. She's pregnant. She's leaving.* 'Er…Okay. You want to go inside?'

'Here's as good a place as any.' She took both of his hands in hers and looked up at him, those large blue eyes shimmering. After a deep breath that she let out slowly, she spoke. 'Jack, I know I said that I wasn't looking for anything serious. That those kisses, that this…us—' she pointed to him and then back at her chest '—doesn't mean anything…'

He knew what was coming. The one thing he'd vowed he would never let happen. He couldn't speak. Didn't know what to say.

'But it does. It means something to me.' She bit her lip and there was so much hope in her eyes—hope that he desperately did not want to squash. 'Jack, I'm falling in love with you.'

He turned away. A rock lodged itself in his throat. Of

all the goddamned stupid things to let her do. 'That's a big leap from *this doesn't mean anything.*'

'Well, I know, but it's true.'

He faced her again, words falling from his mouth before he could stop them 'You can't, Cass. You can't.'

'I can. And I can't seem to stop it.'

'Didn't I just tell you what happened to me? Didn't you get from that that I don't do this?'

Her mouth twitched and for a moment he thought she was going to cry but she controlled it. 'I know, but I thought—'

'That you'd try to fix me? Make me feel better?' His voice rose and he knew he was breaking her precious heart. But it was better to do this now than later down the track. Better to let her go than pretend he could love her too, the way she wanted. The way every woman expected. The way she deserved. The way he didn't know how. Jeez, what the hell was he supposed to do now? 'I'm sorry, Cassie. But you've got the wrong man.'

Then he pressed his hand over hers and opened the gate, his instinct telling him to run, to not be taken in by another grand gesture that promised him things he could never have. His mouth dried up from panic; his heartbeat pounded in his ears, steady at first but turning to white noise.

And yet she was the most beautiful thing he'd ever seen, large blue eyes telling him what she couldn't find words to say. A body that he knew so intimately and that he could never tire of kissing. And her smart, funny mouth that showed him how intelligent she really was, how passionate, how dazzling.

But not for him.

He knew she expected more but he didn't know what. She couldn't love him, just like he couldn't love her. End of. No argument. He would not let his hopes be raised and dashed again. Or hers. Definitely not hers. He'd stuffed up the first time he'd kissed her, but he'd just kept coming back for more and let himself get too involved. Pretending he could do this without developing any feelings for her. And worse, that she would not be lulled into thinking he could give her what she needed.

There were tears in her eyes now, but he knew that she was strong enough to not let them fall. That she was strong enough to move on. It was he who had the flaws, not Cassie. She was nothing short of perfect. 'You deserve more, Cassie. From someone who can do this. Not from me.'

'So, how do you feel—about me?' Her chin jutted out and her gaze was almost disdainful.

'Confused, right now. Blindsided, to be honest.' He should have watched for the signs instead of listening to her telling him she wasn't crazy and didn't want anything more.

She laughed, bitter and sharp. 'You didn't see it coming? After everything we've shared, everything we've done, you didn't think I'd develop feelings for you? Even a little bit?'

'Of course.' He should have known that not everyone was as controlled as he was. And yet *confused* was the only way to describe how he felt. She *loved* him. That was big. It did mean something. No one had ever said that to him before. Not even Lizzie. No one.

How the hell was he supposed to react? He wasn't going to lie to her and swear happy everlasting for ever—he wasn't going to promise her stuff he didn't believe in. 'I… Don't know. I kind of thought that it wouldn't get this far.'

And now Cassie felt like a royal twit. A stupid, pathetic, soppy, hearts and flowers sap—the one thing she'd promised never to be. Forgetting herself and laying her heart out like that for him to stamp on. *Not this sister.*

Staring into his eyes, she looked for something, anything, that told her he felt the same, but he'd slipped back that mask—the one that hid his emotions. Back to his normal, his usual. Cold and alone.

Her heart felt as if it were crumbling. But she was the one who'd broken the rules; she'd let her heart get messed up by him. He'd always been honest and open about where things could go and what he was prepared to give. But somehow it had become more than either of them had expected.

She wasn't going to beg and she didn't look like she was about to change his mind any time soon. But, more, she wasn't about to let him know how much she was stung by this rejection. 'Well, at least you didn't nick my stuff, so that's a bonus. Okay, well, I'll just go in and get my things.'

'Wait, I'll give you a hand.'

'I can manage.' *Just leave me alone.*

But it was his house; he followed up the path. How different this time, as she wandered through his garden, when she went into his empty house. His revelations about his past had explained a lot. Why he didn't have family stuff, or even anything resembling a home. The guy didn't know how.

He knew how to compartmentalise his feelings so he wouldn't get hurt again. Knew where to draw the line before things got difficult. And she'd thought she'd managed to do the same, but he'd grown on her. He might not have stolen her stuff, but he'd definitely stolen a part of her heart.

The beautiful, infuriating, grumpy bastard.

The kitchen was as messy as her head, but together they scooped up the dirty containers and loaded her boxes, ran a sink of scalding water and slid in the pans. Filled the dishwasher. Wiped the counters. Washed down the table, where only a few hours ago he'd been making love to her, where she'd given herself to him—and, she'd believed, he'd given himself to her.

And now she was just that little bit less. She fought back the tears.

He saw her to the door. 'Okay, then, well, I'll see you at the wedding.'

'You bet.'

'Don't be late, eh?'

'Me? Never.' She winked, unable to say any more past the lump wedged in her throat.

'Wait.' He ran his thumb along her mouth; even now, desire clouded his eyes. Then he pressed a kiss on her cheek, so gentle and tender it made her heart almost stop. And even after the humiliation of laying her soul bare, her body still ached for him, wanted his kisses, wanted his touch to linger, wanted him to piece her shattered heart back together. 'Bye, Cassie. I'm sorry.'

'Yeah, me too.'

He looked away then, his throat moving as he swallowed, his rigid self-control slipping just a little. And that was what made this so damn hard. He had feelings for her, she knew; he liked her, he wanted her, it just wasn't enough to break through that hardened heart.

CHAPTER TWELVE

'This is really good. Better than good—you've captured exactly the feeling I was trying to get—it's not too voy-euristic, but it showcases Jono's emotions really well.' Jack stood and made to leave the cutting room but turned back to Billy. Fair's fair, the man deserved some praise. 'You've impressed me no end this week; this is really shaping up. Thanks. Thanks a lot. I'm going to get off home now. You should too.'

'Cheers, boss. Have a good wedding.' Billy grinned and pinked up from ear to ear. Then turned back to the screen and started pressing buttons, too polite to tell his boss what a jerk he'd been.

Leaving Billy to get on with his job had been brilliant. One of Cassie's better suggestions, for which Jack needed to thank her. His new editor had come up with some great ideas and had almost finished the job, which was just as well because Jack had had nothing forthcoming. Staring at the screen and seeing Cassie's heartbroken face reflected back hadn't helped. Neither had drowning his thoughts in beer. Or trying to work into the night to forget her.

Nothing had helped.

He missed her.

Walking out into the large wide corridor overlooking the Thames, he stared down at the boats and ant-sized people. Everyone going about their daily business. Living their lives. Scuttling around. He thought about where Cassie might be—at her flat, prepping for tomorrow, at a job somewhere, in that wreck of a van. Wherever she was, she'd be causing someone a great deal of chaos, and bringing them a hell of a lot of joy too. How could she not?

A sharp ache twisted in his chest—seemed he couldn't get rid of it. Get rid of the idea of her. The two things were interlinked. The more he missed her, the more he actually, physically hurt. She'd left her smell imprinted on his house, on his clothes. Her voice still rang loud in his head, and as he looked around, everywhere he went, he wanted to catch a glimpse of her colour, of her mess.

Loved her? That he didn't know. It was too big a call for him. He'd never used the word and to him it had always seemed something too far out of reach.

He made his way outside into the sunshine, hailed a cab. Drove across town, made the taxi-driver swing by Cassie's street just to catch sight of her house.

And if that wasn't pathetic he didn't know what was. He didn't know how to make things right, whether he could. Whether he had the guts to even try. Because that was what it needed, in the end: hard work, guts and a lot of belief. He could do the first, but he stumbled on the second two.

When the taxi drew up outside his destination he saw a bright smiling face waiting for him in the doorway, such light in her eyes, excitement thrumming from every pore. He paid the cab, jumped out and gave her a kiss on the cheek, and his heart did a little leap. 'Hey. Sorry to keep you waiting.'

'Jack! Jack, where've you been? Hurry up. We're just ordering.' Lizzie ushered him inside the restaurant and he fixed his brotherly smile. Yes, he was looking forward to tomorrow. Of course he'd picked his suit up. Yes, he'd make sure he was there early.

Wow, his sister was getting married. The feeling kind of choked him a little. The end of an era.

After dinner, Lizzie took his arm and walked him to a quiet part of the bar. Given that there was a band starting up, that was no mean feat. She put her hand on his chest. 'Hey, big brother of mine. Are you okay? You're not your usual self tonight.'

He found her a smile, not wanting to ruin her big event. 'Of course I'm okay; my little sister looks so happy, and she's getting married tomorrow—I feel great. About time someone took you off my hands. I've just a lot on my mind.'

'Let me guess.' She pretended to think for a moment. 'The global financial crisis? Hmm. No. World peace? I'm guessing not. A certain redheaded chef who makes a mean roti and dances like...well, like nobody's watching? Getting hotter?'

'No.'

'Come on, Jack, even the mention of her and your whole manner changes.'

'What do you mean?' He tried to stand his normal way. Whatever that was.

She laughed. 'Don't think I haven't realised. Seeing you with Cassie at the Carnival. You like her. She clearly likes you, so what's the problem?'

'There is no problem.'

'She's left you? Oh, God—is she still coming tomorrow?' Her hand at her mouth, she winced. 'Sorry, callous.'

'She'll be there. Probably late, but there it is.' He rubbed his temples with his fingertips. Inside him, his gut was like a human washing machine. If he couldn't tell Lizzie, then he might as well self-destruct right now. 'I don't know what to do.'

'What? Jack, who has all the answers finally hasn't got one?' She stroked his back. 'Poor baby. Do you love her?'

'You know me. I don't do that. I can't—'

She shook her head. 'You *didn't*. I didn't even know how to love myself. Neither of us could, not for a long time. But Jack, you love me, you took care of me, you gave up so much and gave me more. You can love someone else; you have to give it a try…or what's the point of everything we went through? You deserve to love someone, and for them to love you back.'

He closed his eyes. What did it mean to love someone? That pieces of him fitted together when Cassie was around? That she made him smile. That the part of his heart that had been closed off felt wide open and full at the same time when he looked at her. That her touch made him feel wanted and needed, excited yet comfortable.

Comfortable. His eyes slammed open again; he'd been there before, too many times, and had his hopes shattered again and again. 'But what if—?'

Lizzie put her finger over his lips. 'No. Whatever happens, Jack, you'll survive it. Hey, what if it does work out? What if you're happy? Just allow yourself to consider that that might happen. Look at me and Callum—that wasn't easy; I didn't want to fall in love with him but the annoying Irish devil persuaded me.' She looked up into his face; the smile that once upon a time he didn't think he'd ever see again shone from her. 'Tell her.'

'I don't know. I don't know.' He didn't know what to do or say. Ever since Cassie had dropped the L word bombshell he'd been flailing around, trying to find a name for what he was feeling. He'd thought that walking away was the easier thing to do but it wasn't. Living every day without her was harder. Damned hard. He didn't want to do it any more, but he didn't know what to do to make it right.

'You know, I'm not sure if I've ever said it out loud, but I love you, Jack. I love you. Thank you, big brother, you saved me.' Lizzie pressed a kiss onto his cheek. 'Now, go save yourself.'

'Jeez, no one says I love you for twenty-eight years and then two women say it within a week.' Maybe there was something in the water. Maybe Lizzie was right. Maybe he could do it. He'd managed to bring up his sister and win awards for a career he'd carved out for himself every painful step of the way. Not being afraid of any barriers, he'd managed a successful life on his own. Yeah, on his own—successful in one aspect and woefully unsuccessful in the part that mattered most.

He'd shied away from emotional connection for so long he hadn't seen it coming, believed he could control that along with everything else. But the one thing he'd learnt was that control and Cassie were direct opposites.

The thought of her made his heart thrill and ache.

Maybe it was time he took a leaf out of her book and looked into his heart, and was truly honest about what he saw. Surely he could tell a woman how he felt instead of hiding behind decades-old wounds? Surely he could risk his battered heart for her? Because if she wasn't worth that, then no one was.

'Not again. Not again. Not again.' Cassie pulled up outside the art gallery and breathed out, resisting a sharp toot on the horn to announce her arrival. 'No, sirree! Not late again. Not even on time, but early. Stick that in your pipe, Jack Bloody Brennan.'

What the hell was she doing? It was sheer madness, coming here to face him again after the humiliation of last week, but she'd made a promise to Lizzie and Callum and she never ever reneged on her promises.

Still, she took a moment to compose herself before she had to walk in and give him a cheery *I don't care if you broke my heart* smile. *I'm fine.* Because she would be, soon. Although, if the last seven days were anything to go by, soon wasn't soon enough. The man had thrown her love back in her face and, even though she'd survived other things—losing her hard-earned cash, losing her trust, losing her father—losing Jack was so very, very hard. Every day she woke up with him on her mind, every night she wished she were lying in his arms.

She wished she was wearing something more killer than a chef outfit. That dress from the awards night, for instance. Something more feminine. Just to show him what he was missing. Still, nothing beat a happy smile and a sharp tongue. She climbed out of the van, lifted out some boxes and knocked on the gallery door.

Callum opened it and ushered her into the cavernous space that had been transformed from a dreary soulless room into a magical wedding venue. Metres and metres of white muslin draped like canopies across the ceiling, fairy lights hung at intervals, shedding sparkling white light over the central area. White wooden chairs were set out in one large circle, each with a simple posy of giant daisies attached to the back. In the middle of the circle were two chairs with white velvet cushions. It was so pure, and breathtaking. Cassie's throat filled. 'Wow. It's gorgeous.'

Callum nodded. 'She's done a grand job, my Lizzie. She's also brought her food contribution; it's in the kitchen. I'll give you a hand getting things sorted. Kick off's in a couple of hours or so.'

Which gave Cassie one hundred and twenty minutes

to summon calm before her body and brain went into mind melt.

Or, rather, continued on the mind melt downward trajectory. She took a deep breath, grateful that Jack wasn't here, and tried to concentrate on her job.

And where the hell did that time go? Before she could turn around, the place had started to fill with well-dressed guests, laughing and catching their breath as they stepped into the fairy tale that Lizzie had made. Cassie sent out the two catering students with trays of cocktails and hoped upon hope that Jack wouldn't seek her out in the kitchen.

But then the band started up with a jazzy version of *Here Comes the Bride* and she just couldn't resist sticking her nose out to sneak a look. Before she could stop herself, her hand hit her mouth at the sight of the two siblings walking down the petal-strewn aisle into the circle, Lizzie so radiant in her flowing strapless gown and Jack… her heart stalled…so proud and tall and beautiful in his dark suit and tamed hair.

She managed to stop herself from running forward and messing it up, just a little, the only out of control thing about a man so in control. She thought that for a moment he might have looked towards her, but she dipped her eyes away, not wanting to let him see what she knew was still in her eyes. Her love for him.

The wedding was conducted in the circle—a ring within a ring. Such a fitting idea, and then, after tears and wonderful vows, the chairs were cleared to the sides of the room and the band was starting up again. Cassie was kept busy with canapés and the buffet, the cutting of the cake. Speeches. Again, more tears. Applause. General chit-chat and photographs, Jack deep in conversation with a couple, a shorter guy with a beard, the woman pregnant and blooming.

And still Cassie's eyes followed his back and hid from his gaze. She returned to the kitchen, pulled on her rubber gloves and started to wash up, happy that Lizzie had finally got her fairy tale.

One day...

No. She couldn't think like that. One wedding and she'd started to believe in it? No, Jack's rejection had made her even more determined that she would not fall for it all again.

'Cassie.' His warm deep voice made her jump, made her hands tremble. She turned around; he'd removed his tie and loosened his shirt top button, damn the man. Did he have to be so startling?

'Hi.' She pressed her lips together. What to say to the man who you'd humiliated yourself in front of? Ordinarily, she'd have told him where to get off, but here, now? That would not go down well at a wedding. Plus, he was paying the bill.

'Jack.' *Lame.*

'I need to talk to you. But first I need to know the paring knife is under lock and key.'

She pursed her lips. 'Your lucky day, mate. I didn't bring it; too much blood does tend to cause a downer on a wedding day.' She held up the sudsy gloves. 'I'd offer for you to join me, but I don't have any your size.' *In other words: go away.*

Undeterred, he stepped into the room, his hands thrust deep in his pockets. He looked sheepish, which was a first for the usually over-confident Jack. 'I'm a jerk.'

Her heart thumped. 'Oh, yes, I'm well aware of that.'

'But I want to try to make amends.'

She steadied herself. The guy was just being nice, because she knew that underneath he was actually an honourable man. So it was annoying that her body had gone into full-on prickly heat hope. 'I'm waiting.'

'You see that guy out there—beard, pregnant wife?' He pointed to the short man from before. What? Strange apology style, but anyway...

'Yes?'

'He's the top dog at the Peregrine film studio in Shepherd's Bush and he needs a caterer. I've told him about you. Expect a call, and a contract to follow shortly after.'

The prickly heat turned into hives. Her anger started to boil up from the pit in her stomach, mixed with humiliation and outright love for the self-confessed jerk. 'Are you for real? That's how you make amends? By striding in and doing exactly what I don't want you to do? Interfering? Taking over? Did you even think of asking me?'

His hands raised, palm up, to calm her, his voice soothing and low. 'Hey, I wanted to help you. You were trying so hard.'

So difficult to argue in a stage whisper. Outside, the happy couple were chatting to guests, blithely oblivious to World War Three raging in the kitchen—lucky them. 'Have you not listened to anything I've said?'

He shook his head. 'Just wait right on here. You said word of mouth works better. You said recommendation is the best way of getting jobs.'

'Yes, but not from you and not just to make yourself feel better.'

'It's not to make me feel better; it's to help you. Why is it okay for Lizzie to recommend you—which, by the way, she did—and he then came to find me because you were busy, and it's good enough for head injury girl. But not me?'

He had a point. But interfering was so damned annoying. 'But...just stay out of my business.'

'Could it be that perhaps, just perhaps, I think your

food is great? That *he* thinks your food is great? You know what? Forgive me for having a conversation. Forgive me for praising you. And forgive me for being so damned in love with you that I might have been a little excited that Mr Big out there wants a regular contractor, which will mean big bucks for you. Forget the whole damned thing. Go find your own contracts. I'm done arguing.' He raked a hand across his hair.

Hallelujah—messed up hair. Finally! In a tuxedo…and his eyes, so sexy… Now she was in trouble. Big… Wait… 'So damned in love?'

He didn't look overly thrilled at the prospect, his eyebrows furrowed. 'Yes. It appears so.'

Out in the art gallery, the first dance had started, something lilting and soft. From where she was standing, she could see Lizzie wrapped in Callum's arms, staring up into his eyes, full of love. And here, the eyes of her brother looked the same. But how could she believe him?

She lowered her voice even more, stepping closer to him just so she could smell…rather, just so she could make herself understood. 'Double jerk. Don't come in here and say that. Don't try to fix my problems and come in here… don't tell me you love me.'

'If it's the truth, then why not?' He stepped a little closer too, pausing to clip back her stupid loose curl—the way he used to with his sister. Her chest suddenly got tight.

Because…she couldn't think of any reason why not. Because she couldn't bear it if he walked away. He'd already done that and it would hurt too much to let it happen again. But then, hadn't he given her so much already—shown her how he felt, even if he couldn't say it? Hadn't he rescued her, helped her, cared for her? The way he made love to her was not—could not have been—a pretence of affection. Mr Grumpy wasn't that good an actor.

'I *need* it to be true, Jack.'

'You surprised me and I didn't know how to handle that, or the feelings I have. I've spent all my life trying not to get involved because I know how hard it is to recover from broken promises. From thrashed hope. So I tried to control my feelings for you like I control everything else in my life. But…well, you grew on me. You taught me how to embrace life, how to live. To be free and have fun along the way. I was doing great in my soulless, colourless life, thank you very much. But you're so strong and independent and vibrant—you made my life into a damned rainbow— and now I can't imagine living without you. I've never said this to another soul, ever. I've never believed I could say it, and now you've made me believe I can. I love you.'

'Oh.' Her chest grew so tight she didn't think she could breathe. 'I—'

'Brilliant. Speechless. Excellent. Now I know how to shut you up. I love you. I love you.'

Her whole body felt as if it was smiling—she'd never say another word again if it meant she could hear that voice say those words.

The music played on and on; he took her rubber-gloved hand in his. 'You want to dance?'

'Like this?' Oops, talking. She couldn't help herself. She held up her gloves and indicated her chef's whites. 'I'm supposed to be working.'

His hand was on her waist and he was pulling her to him. 'Who cares? Nobody's watching.'

'I don't know, Jack.' She pulled away a little; it was too easy to get carried away, but she wanted to be so utterly honest that he knew exactly what he was getting into. 'I think I was wrong. I think I do want the fairy tale and I know you don't want to give me that.'

Pressing a kiss on her head, he asked in a voice so dark

and deep she wanted to never stop hearing him, 'Which one? Which fairy tale do you want?'

'Just the one with the happy ever after.'

He took a very deep breath and then let it go, and with it he began to smile. He tilted her chin up so he could look her in the eyes, and there she saw it all. His love, his honour, his commitment. 'Then that's the one you'll have. At least, I'll do my best. If that's good enough?'

Good enough? He was doing the one thing for her that he'd never believed was possible—loving her, offering her a future. Her throat was thick and raw. 'Absolutely. I love you too, Jack Brennan.'

'Now, dance with me. I happen to find yellow rubber gloves very sexy.'

'Well, in that case...' Cassie fitted herself into his heat, the soft music pulsing a rhythm she felt through her body as she moved against him. His grip on her was solid but restrained, gentle yet assured. All words lost. Only intent. She wanted to feel him, to touch him. His mouth was mere inches from hers and all she could see was his face so close. So beautiful. So intense. His breath warm along her skin. His eyes heavy with a need that she knew was matched in her gaze.

When he lowered his head to hers and his mouth touched her lips she melted against him, lost herself in his kiss, in his arms. A place she never wanted to leave.

When he finally pulled away, he smiled that glorious Jack smile that had become more heart-warming, more welcome than the sun coming up. 'I love you, Cass. I want you so much.' His mouth was on her neck now, breathing promises of more heat, more fun, more love to come. 'And I particularly want some more of that rum and butter sauce...'

She pressed against him, wondering if anything could

beat the feeling she had right now—she sorely doubted it. 'If you kiss me like that again, Jack Brennan, you can have anything you want.'

* * * * *

Mills & Boon® Hardback

April 2014

ROMANCE

0314GEN STD HB

Mills & Boon® Large Print
April 2014

ROMANCE

Defiant in the Desert	Sharon Kendrick
Not Just the Boss's Plaything	Caitlin Crews
Rumours on the Red Carpet	Carole Mortimer
The Change in Di Navarra's Plan	Lynn Raye Harris
The Prince She Never Knew	Kate Hewitt
His Ultimate Prize	Maya Blake
More than a Convenient Marriage?	Dani Collins
Second Chance with Her Soldier	Barbara Hannay
Snowed in with the Billionaire	Caroline Anderson
Christmas at the Castle	Marion Lennox
Beware of the Boss	Leah Ashton

HISTORICAL

Not Just a Wallflower	Carole Mortimer
Courted by the Captain	Anne Herries
Running from Scandal	Amanda McCabe
The Knight's Fugitive Lady	Meriel Fuller
Falling for the Highland Rogue	Ann Lethbridge

MEDICAL

Gold Coast Angels: A Doctor's Redemption	Marion Lennox
Gold Coast Angels: Two Tiny Heartbeats	Fiona McArthur
Christmas Magic in Heatherdale	Abigail Gordon
The Motherhood Mix-Up	Jennifer Taylor
The Secret Between Them	Lucy Clark
Craving Her Rough Diamond Doc	Amalie Berlin

0314 GEN STD LP

Mills & Boon® Hardback
May 2014

ROMANCE

The Only Woman to Defy Him	Carol Marinelli
Secrets of a Ruthless Tycoon	Cathy Williams
Gambling with the Crown	Lynn Raye Harris
The Forbidden Touch of Sanguardo	Julia James
One Night to Risk it All	Maisey Yates
A Clash with Cannavaro	Elizabeth Power
The Truth About De Campo	Jennifer Hayward
Sheikh's Scandal	Lucy Monroe
Beach Bar Baby	Heidi Rice
Sex, Lies & Her Impossible Boss	Jennifer Rae
Lessons in Rule-Breaking	Christy McKellen
Twelve Hours of Temptation	Shoma Narayanan
Expecting the Prince's Baby	Rebecca Winters
The Millionaire's Homecoming	Cara Colter
The Heir of the Castle	Scarlet Wilson
Swept Away by the Tycoon	Barbara Wallace
Return of Dr Maguire	Judy Campbell
Heatherdale's Shy Nurse	Abigail Gordon

MEDICAL

200 Harley Street: The Proud Italian	Alison Roberts
200 Harley Street: American Surgeon in London	Lynne Marshall
A Mother's Secret	Scarlet Wilson
Saving His Little Miracle	Jennifer Taylor

Mills & Boon® Large Print
May 2014

ROMANCE

The Dimitrakos Proposition	Lynne Graham
His Temporary Mistress	Cathy Williams
A Man Without Mercy	Miranda Lee
The Flaw in His Diamond	Susan Stephens
Forged in the Desert Heat	Maisey Yates
The Tycoon's Delicious Distraction	Maggie Cox
A Deal with Benefits	Susanna Carr
Mr (Not Quite) Perfect	Jessica Hart
English Girl in New York	Scarlet Wilson
The Greek's Tiny Miracle	Rebecca Winters
The Final Falcon Says I Do	Lucy Gordon

HISTORICAL

From Ruin to Riches	Louise Allen
Protected by the Major	Anne Herries
Secrets of a Gentleman Escort	Bronwyn Scott
Unveiling Lady Clare	Carol Townend
A Marriage of Notoriety	Diane Gaston

MEDICAL

Gold Coast Angels: Bundle of Trouble	Fiona Lowe
Gold Coast Angels: How to Resist Temptation	Amy Andrews
Her Firefighter Under the Mistletoe	Scarlet Wilson
Snowbound with Dr Delectable	Susan Carlisle
Her Real Family Christmas	Kate Hardy
Christmas Eve Delivery	Connie Cox